Ann was born in Watford Hertfordshire and grew up in and around Watford. Ann was educated at the Watford Grammar School for Girls before completing a secretarial course and working in Watford and London as a secretary. At the age of 22 Ann left home to travel overseas through Africa and Asia before returning to England to marry and settle down. Wanderlust struck again when the children were small, and Ann and her husband emigrated to South Australia. They returned to England after seven years to introduce their new son to the family and to live and work in Herefordshire for 18 months before returning to South Australia. Since her husband's death, Ann has resumed her love of travel exploring outback Australia, travelling on the Trans-Siberian Railway and visiting South Africa and England.

For May, my mother, who loved a good laugh.

Ann Clouder

LOVE? IN A COTTAGE

AUSTIN MACAULEY PUBLISHERS™

LONDON • CAMBRIDGE • NEW YORK • SHARJAH

A CIP catalogue record for this title is available from the British Library.

ISBN 9781398483927 (Paperback)
ISBN 9781398483941 (ePub e-book)
ISBN 9781398483934 (Audiobook)

www.austinmacauley.com

First Published 2023
Austin Macauley Publishers Ltd®
1 Canada Square
Canary Wharf
London
E14 5AA

Table of Contents

Synopsis

Love? in a Cottage is a light-hearted book intended to make the reader laugh. It is set in rural Herefordshire in the early 1960s. It has two main characters, Marlene Sugden and Donald Evans. Marlene is a 38-year-old woman who works as a secretary in London. She has been left on her own after the death of her father and her life has changed very much for the worse. Marlene finally in desperation, decides to advertise for a husband in the 'Lonely Hearts' column of the Evening Standard.

Donald Evans is a man in his forties who is in a similar situation to Marlene, having been left to live on his own in his late thirties after the death of his mother. Donald has been actively seeking a wife amongst the local women of the Herefordshire village in which he lives, but none will look at him as he is renowned for his meanness. He has a pleasant but sadly neglected stone cottage with a few acres of land, and he earns his living by working on the surrounding farms and properties on a casual basis.

Donald reads Marlene's advertisement in an old newspaper which he has picked up and brought home to tear up and use for toilet paper. He decides to reply to the advertisement and Marlene, after one unhappy meeting with a London man, writes to Donald. After some correspondence they meet in Aylesbury twice before they arrange for Marlene to visit Donald's cottage.

Marlene visits the cottage one sunny day in late autumn day and is very happy with what she sees. The cottage is shabby and in need of a coat of paint and a good clean, but she sees nothing that she cannot put right. The only drawback as far as Marlene is concerned is the lack of plumbing and proper toilet facilities. Over a cup of tea Marlene and Donald discuss the possibility of their marriage and Marlene agrees that she will marry Donald provided that he 'lays on the water' to the cottage. By this Marlene has in mind a proper bathroom and flush toilet but as she later discovers Donald put a very different interpretation on the words. Marlene does not see the cottage again until after she has become Mrs Donald Evans.

Marlene seriously considers abandoning her marriage but decides to persevere. She learns how to grow vegetables and keep poultry, to cook on a wood stove and to outwit Donald and to extract money from him for essentials such as proper toilet paper. Donald for his part is more than content with Marlene's cooking and the improvements in his life and for many months lives on tenterhooks in case Marlene should decide to return to her life in London, although he does at times regret having married 'a London woman'. A good Herefordshire girl would have been far more understanding – if only he had been able to find one willing to marry him.

Disclaimer

All the characters in *Love? In A Cottage* are imaginary and are not based on the lives of any person, living or dead. This book is entirely a work of fiction set in the beautiful rural county of Herefordshire in the 1960s.

Ann Clouder

Chapter One
The Advertisement

Marlene stepped down from the railway carriage as the train pulled into the station and hurried up the steps to the road, pulling her coat around her against the chilly evening breeze. Her heels tapped as she walked briskly along the road and then took a short cut through the park. She cast an idle glance at a pair of lovers laying in the grass, their bodies entwined closely and wondered for a moment what it would be like to be so close to another person. At last she crossed the High Street and took the lane down the side of the Odeon Cinema, which was showing Gregory Peck in *Roman Holiday*. She had been planning to have an early supper and see the film again this evening but that was out of the question now as she was so late home.

Marlene turned the key in her front door, stepped into the tiny hallway and listened to the silence. The flat was exactly as she had left it that morning, quiet and neat and empty. She went to her bedroom to hang up her coat and tidy her hair. As she looked in the mirror, she convinced herself she could see new wrinkles on her face. This morning she had pulled out another three grey hairs. She walked through into the kitchen, dropped her parcels on the table and put the kettle on for a cup of tea. She sighed despondently. How she hated living alone but what could she do about it?

Marlene had been on her own now for eighteen months, ever since her father had died. Her mother had died many years ago when Marlene was a teenager and Marlene had cared for her father devotedly. They had lived very happily together, both working and enjoying each other's company and since her father's death Marlene had been very a lonely woman. Her best friend, Joyce, had married six months ago and had immediately emigrated to Australia with her new husband. Their only contact now was by letter. To cap it all John Smythe, her boss for the last 15 years, had retired. Marlene had had a very happy working relationship with him, and she found her new boss, a snappy short-tempered man, hard to get on with. He had kept Marlene back this evening altering letters where he had changed his mind, and this was what had caused her to miss her usual train. Marlene suspected that he was deliberately making her life difficult so that she would leave, and he could employ a pretty young blonde in her place.

In her earlier years, her father had discouraged any attempt on her part to find a partner and since his death she had tried many ways of meeting eligible men of her own age. She had tried evening classes, joined a social club and even made one disastrous foray to a nightclub on her own but her gawky shyness made making friends difficult. Being 5'9" tall, with large hands and feet and a long bony face, didn't help as any man who asked her to dance was invariably several inches shorter than Marlene when they stood up together. But beneath this somewhat plain exterior was a kindhearted, loving and intelligent woman who was a gifted cook and homemaker, a woman who desperately wanted a husband and home to love and care for and who was prepared to try almost anything to find him.

Marlene made the tea and sat sipping it as she turned the pages of the evening paper, pausing to read here and there. She glanced at the crossword and put it on one side to tackle later. Maybe she should look for a new job. She turned the pages looking for the situations vacant advertisements when the Lonely Hearts column caught her eye. Here were men seeking women 'for companionship view matrimony' and women seeking men. Was it worth a try?

Marlene found a pen and paper and sat down to draft an advertisement. She thought hard. What did she really want in a man? He would have to be kind, single and not too old and in need of a good wife. How could you put that in an advertisement? How about:

Lonely unmarried woman, late 30's, good cook and homemaker seeks kind-hearted single middle-aged man view matrimony if suited.

That was it! She would take it in to the front office of the paper tomorrow and pay for a Box Number for replies to be sent to. Yes, she would do it before her courage failed her. The decision made; Marlene set about preparing her evening meal in a more cheerful frame of mind.

Chapter Two
The Reply

Deep in the heart of rural Herefordshire Donald Evans parked his bike against the wall of his cottage, slipped off his wellingtons and lifted the latch to go into the kitchen. He could tell by the chill in the air as soon as he went in that the wood stove had gone out again. He would have to tie some holly in a bunch and pull it down the chimney to clear the soot that was blocking it.

He went into the pantry in his stockinged feet, a toe poking through one sock and a heel gleaming through a hole in the other and came out with a tin of baked beans, a loaf of bread and some butter. He opened the tin of beans and settled down at the kitchen table to make a simple meal while browsing through a two-day old evening paper that he had found in a bin at The Larches. Donald had never in his life spent good money on buying a newspaper when it was possible to get a day old one for free. Donald was eating the beans straight from the tin with a spoon as he turned the pages of the paper, reading here and there, when the Lonely-Hearts column caught his eye. He read Marlene's advertisement, paused, and read it again. Donald had been trying to find a wife for years. His situation was similar to Marlene's. His father had been killed in a tractor accident when Donald was in his early twenties and he had taken over the running of the small holding, living with his mother and being perfectly content with life until his mother had died of pneumonia, after a bout of the flu, leaving Donald on his own.

For the last five years Donald had been searching for a wife but as he was renowned for his meanness the women of the district had steered clear of him. Donald had thought he was in with a chance with the barmaid of The Bear's Head at Withington. She had visited his cottage and suggested that she might be interested if Donald had the cottage wired for electricity. After carefully considering the benefits of a wife against the cost of the electricity Donald had had the cottage wired – only to see the barmaid marry a long-distance lorry driver from Cardiff.

Donald considered the advertisement. He was single, middle-aged, yes, and kindhearted too if it didn't cost him anything. He was desperately in need of a good cook and homemaker as the cottage had fallen into a sad state since his mother had died. It would only cost him the price of a stamp to answer the advertisement for there was some old notepaper in the dresser he could use. He would reply tonight, it was worth a try.

When Donald arrived home that evening, he cooked himself some sausage and egg, put the dishes in the sink, sorted out the cleanest piece of notepaper and hunted high and low for a pen. It was no good, the only biro he could find just wouldn't write so it had to be a pencil. He licked the tip of it and started to write.

Dear Madam,

I have read your advertisement for a husband in the paper. I would like to apply for the job. I am unmarried, in my early forties and consider myself to be kind-hearted. I have been on my own now for five years since my dear mother died. I have a small cottage and a few acres of land. I keeps a few cows and some hens and grows all my own vegetables. I do a bit of work around the place to keep the money coming in. If you should be interested in my application maybe, we could meet. I would be happy to come to London if it would suit you better.

Yours truly
Donald Evans

Donald read the letter through and wished that he hadn't put that he would like to 'apply for the job'. Too late to change it now, though, he had written in indelible pencil so it wouldn't rub out and there was no more clean writing paper. Then he realised that he hadn't written his address, so he carefully squeezed it in at the top. 'Stone House, Millbrook, Near Micklebury, Hfds.' He addressed the envelope, stuck on the stamp he had bought earlier in the day and walked into the village to post the letter before he changed his mind.

There were fors and againsts an arrangement like this he thought. On the one hand she wouldn't know anything about him, but, then again, he wouldn't know anything about her. He slipped the letter into the box and drifted into the Red Lion for a quiet half of bitter and a game of darts before he went home to bed. If nothing came of this it had only cost him the price of a stamp, and he would dearly love a good cook and homemaker in his little cottage. He wondered what the woman meant by 'good cook'? He had better find out before matters went too far. Donald was not a person who worried about his waistline and starved himself. He wouldn't be interested in any of these newfangled ideas about not eating butter and chips and a good roast.

Chapter Three
A Meeting

Marlene waited for five days before she went into the offices of the Evening Standard to collect the replies to her advertisement. She went in her lunch hour, tucked the envelopes well out of sight in her handbag and didn't look at them again until she reached home that night. She made herself her usual cup of tea and spread the envelopes, 14 of them, on the table. With shaking hands she started to open them, her face flushing red then white as she ripped one letter, containing a pornographic photo, into little pieces before consigning it to the bin. Many of the letters were from older men, up to 75 years of age, who considered themselves 'young in heart', one or two quite openly said that they didn't really want a wife but would be happy to offer Marlene a very good position as a live in housekeeper, and three of the letters were from men in their forties who appeared to be in similar circumstances to Marlene and genuinely sought companionship and marriage. Marlene put these three on one side. She did not want to consider any man over fifty as she felt that she would all too soon find herself in the same circumstances again, nursing an elderly man and then having the heartbreak of being left alone.

Marlene laid the letters from the three possible applicants out before her and sipped her tea thoughtfully. One letter came from a single man, living in the London area, a bachelor with a good job and a car. He sounded almost too good to be true. The next was from a widower who lived north of Inverness and had three teenaged children, something that Marlene had not really considered. She had little to do with children, being an only child herself, and she seldom came into contact with them in the course of her work. She found the idea of becoming a stepmother to three teenagers somewhat daunting.

The third letter puzzled Marlene. It was the only letter written in pencil and it was written on a somewhat grubby piece of notepaper, but the idea of living in the country with hens and cows and a vegetable plot was something that Marlene had always dreamed of doing. She fingered the letter thoughtfully before putting it on one side.

Marlene prepared her evening meal, cleared away the dishes and settled down to read the letters again. Some of the older men sounded attractive, well established with comfortable homes and children off their hands. Maybe she would come back to them if the three 'possibles' were no good. She decided to reply to the letter from the London bachelor. He was the nearest and sounded the most likely person, so she wrote a brief note suggesting a meeting one Saturday or Sunday when he was free. This time she gave her local post office as the return address for she didn't want any strange man landing on her doorstep before she had a chance to check him out.

Two days later his reply was in her hands suggesting that they should meet by Nelson's Column in Trafalgar Square at two o'clock on the following Saturday. He would wear a red carnation in his buttonhole and carry a furled umbrella, and they would go to a nearby cafe for a quiet afternoon tea. He signed himself *'Sincerely yours, Reg'*.

For the next two days Marlene was in a tizz. What should she wear? She arranged to get her hair done on Saturday morning and hunted through her wardrobe for her most becoming outfit. She decided on a navy suit with a pleated white blouse and a pair of low-heeled shoes, just in case he was not a tall man.

At the appointed time she stood nervously by Nelson's Column feeling conspicuous and wishing that she had never thought of this silly idea. She jumped when a voice spoke behind her. 'Are you Miss Marlene Sugden by any chance?'

'Yes,' said Marlene turning to view her suitor for the first time. Her heart sank. Reg was no more than 5'3" tall, prematurely bald with protruding brown eyes. They made their way to the cafe and ordered a pot of tea and scones. Their conversation was stilted and uncomfortable, made more so when Reg, in a misguided effort to warm things up, put his hand on Marlene's knee and began gently stroking it. Marlene lifted his hand off her knee and put it on the table, only to have her hand seized and clasped firmly by Reg.

'I think we will do very well together, my dear,' he said confidently. 'How would you like to come for a picnic by the river tomorrow? We could take a rug and find a nice quiet spot.'

Marlene hastily declined his invitation saying she had arranged to have a day out with her cousin.

'Maybe next week, then,' suggested Reg.

'Maybe,' gasped Marlene. 'I have to go now. I'm meeting a friend at three o'clock to see a film.' She picked up her handbag, put her share of the money for the tea on the table and, before Reg could make any more suggestions, she hurried away.

Marlene bolted down the nearest underground station, made her way home and threw herself down in a chair. She was confused and angry. What was wrong with her if she couldn't cope with a man stroking her knee? Then again, why should he take such liberties at their first meeting? Why had she been born so damned tall? Why had she got herself into this situation in the first place? Why not throw it all up and go and live in a convent? It was several hours before Marlene settled down enough to watch her favourite television programme. The thought that a husband might expect sex in their marriage was not something that she had considered. Marlene had not had a boyfriend since her mother's death. Somehow her father had discouraged any ideas in that direction as he did not want his daughter to marry and leave him on his own.

Eventually, Marlene calmed down sufficiently to pick up Donald's letter. Maybe this man was a better proposition. He was certainly unsophisticated. She would write and ask for a few more details, maybe a photograph, before she went so far as to meet him.

Chapter Four
Correspondence

Thus, it was that three days later Donald received a letter delivered by Mary the Shop, the local postmistress, on her bicycle. For Donald to receive a letter was a rare enough event, for him to receive a letter with a London postmark was enough to make Mary quiver with curiosity. Her curiosity was to remain unsatisfied as Donald was out when she arrived. Donald didn't find the letter for a day or so as he seldom went near the front door mat. It wasn't until he went into Mary's shop to buy a packet of biscuits and Mary started to try and find out who the letter was from that he realised that it was there at all. He paid for the biscuits, mounted his elderly bike and pedalled home only to find his cousin Hugh, locally known as Tater, waiting for him. Tater was a confirmed bachelor two years younger than Donald, a thin-faced, dark haired man who took a keen interest in the goings on in the village. He had a slightly disabled left arm due to an accident during his childhood and consequently lived on the pension and had plenty of time on his hands to make trouble and cause mischief whenever he saw an opportunity.

Tater followed Donald into the house, equally curious to find out about Donald's letter from London, Mary having spread word about it in the village. Poor Donald had been hoping to keep any hint of it from anyone in the village, now they all knew before he had even met the woman.

'What's this I hear about love letters from London, then?' Tater asked. ''Tis all over the village.'

'I haven't seen any letters,' said Donald quite truthfully, 'Don't know what you are going on about.'

Donald went out to the well to pump up some water for a cup of tea, shook up the wood stove and put the kettle on.

'What were you rummaging in my shed for when I came home?' he asked, diverting Tater's attention from the letter.

'I was after a few nails to fix the fence at the back of my place,' said Tater, putting a handful of nails on the table. 'I seem to have run out and the hens is getting out and scratching in Jill Griffith's flowerbeds. If I don't fix it soon, she reckons she is going to round up the lot of them and put them in her deep freeze.' He sighed. 'I wouldn't put it past her either the miserable cow.

Tater picked up his handful of nails. 'Well, I'd better be on my way then, if there's no letters to read. I thought maybe you'd found one of these mail order brides!' He cocked his leg over his equally decrepit old bicycle and pedalled off up the lane. Donald gave a sigh of relief and hurried to find his letter. He polished his National Health glasses and opened the envelope carefully.

Dear Mr Evans,

Further to your letter in reply to my advertisement, I would appreciate receiving more information about you. Perhaps you could answer the following questions:

1. *How old are you?*
2. *Have you ever been married?*
3. *Have you any children?*
4. *How tall are you?*
5. *Are you in good health?*
6. *Do you own your own house?*
7. *Do you have a car?*

Can you please send me a recent photograph of yourself?

For myself, I am 38 years old, unmarried, I have no children, I am in good health, I live in a rented flat but do have some furniture. I do not own or drive a car.

I enclose a photo of myself taken on holiday in the Lake District two years ago.

I am a good cook, mostly in the way of traditional dishes such as steak and kidney pie, jam roly poly, bread and butter pudding, spotted dick and of course roasts and stews as this was the sort of cooking that my father preferred.

I look forward to hearing from you in the near future.

Yours sincerely,
Marlene Sugden

Donald drooled. Steak and kidney pie, spotted dick, stews and roasts! He was hooked. His next problem was how to reply without the whole village getting to know about it. He had no more notepaper and if he went and bought some from Mary, she she'd be on to it like a shot. He would wait until Thursday and buy some when he was in Micklebury for the market. He'd buy a pen too and do a proper job of it. As an afterthought Donald studied the photograph, it was a bit faint and blurry, but she didn't look too bad. He was nothing special to look at himself with his thinning sandy hair and metal framed spectacles, but at 5'8" he was a respectable height. He pondered the problem of a photograph of himself and hunted out a newspaper clipping taken when he had been leading the prize steer at the Micklebury Show. It had been taken four years ago and he looked a bit younger then, with a bit more hair, but she was not to know that. She would find out soon enough if they met. Donald went out to work in his vegetable garden, dreaming happy dreams of delicious roasts and steaming puddings.

Chapter Five
The First Meeting

The correspondence between Donald and Marlene continued and culminated in a suggestion by Marlene that she was prepared to catch the Green Line coach to Aylesbury one Sunday if Donald would meet her there. She would pack a picnic and they could sit in a park somewhere and get to know each other. They arranged for Donald to meet Marlene at the coach station at mid-day on the next Sunday and Marlene would catch the two fifteen coach back to London, an arrangement which suited Donald very well as it meant he would be home in time for the local Sunday evening darts match and wouldn't have to give any awkward explanations for his absence. He had explained the letters away as from an old mate he had met in the army who wanted to look him up again, but Tater in particular was being very inquisitive about them. A confirmed bachelor and woman hater himself Tater would have been alarmed if he had known what Donald was doing and would have counselled him very strongly against any idea of marrying a strange woman.

As the fateful day approached Donald looked over his clothes, selecting the best of his shirts, a woollen tie, checked sports jacket that had seen better days and a pair of corduroy trousers. It took him some time to find a clean and matching pair of socks without a hole. He sponged and pressed the trousers, brushed the jacket, cleaned his best shoes, snipped any straggly bits of hair and swept the mud and hay out of his old pick-up. On the Saturday night he took down his old zinc bathtub, filled it with hot water from the copper and gave himself a good bath, his regular weekly ritual. He washed his hair, cleaned his teeth and even trimmed and cleaned his fingernails. He felt a new man.

For her part Marlene decided on a blouse and skirt with a cardigan and her lightweight mackintosh in case it rained. She too went to extra trouble with her appearance, having her hair set on the Saturday, but deciding against painting her fingernails. It might look too fancy for a woman hoping to become the wife of a countryman.

On Sunday morning Marlene packed a picnic of cheese and tomato and egg and cress sandwiches, sausage rolls, thick slices of fruit cake and a thermos of tea, packing it all neatly in her shopping bag with her picnic beakers and a checked gingham cloth. She dressed in good time and caught the Green Line as arranged. If the meeting was a failure and she didn't like Donald, well she was going to have a pleasant day out anyway and this attitude put her in a cheerful and optimistic frame of mind.

Donald was ready to leave in good time but was hampered as usual by the unexpected appearance of Tater just as he was about to get into the car. Tater's beady eyes didn't miss a detail of Donald's unusually spruce appearance and he was full of questions, but Donald brushed him aside saying he was late already and had to go, leaving Tater aflame with curiosity.

Donald was already waiting at the coach station when the twelve o'clock coach pulled in. He spotted Marlene immediately, recognising her from her photograph, and felt shy about approaching her. He hadn't come all this way for nothing though, so he walked across to her. Marlene saw him coming and sighed with relief, at least he was taller than Reg and looked quite presentable. She smiled and held out her hand.

'Hello Donald, how nice to meet you at last.'

Donald shook her hand awkwardly and asked if she had a good journey from London.

'Let's go and find a park where we can sit and talk,' said Marlene and they drove around until they found a shady seat in a quiet park. They were both surreptitiously looking each other over as they talked, each happy with what they saw. Marlene was pleased that Donald was clean and quietly spoken and his hands didn't stray over her knees. For his part Donald found Marlene younger and prettier than he had expected. He was more than contented with the contents of the picnic basket for Marlene had unwittingly hit on two all-time favourites of Donald's, sausage rolls and rich fruitcake.

The time passed quickly with Marlene telling Donald about her life as a secretary in London and Donald describing his life in rural Herefordshire. Donald, feeling warm and relaxed after the picnic, talked about his cottage and began to describe the vegetable garden.

'Mind you 'em cwusts be flennen 'ell out me cabbages,' he said conversationally.

Marlene sat bolt upright and looked at him with alarm.

'I didn't think to ask, I just assumed you were English!' she said, blushing and flustered.

'Of course I'm English I'm Herefordshire born and bred,' said Donald, puzzled at her reaction, 'I'm a pedigree whiteface, all I said was the pigeons are tearing me cabbages to shreds.'

Marlene sighed with relief and began to pack away the picnic. As Donald drove back to the bus station they arranged to meet again in a month's time in the same way, and they parted company, both happy with the success of their first meeting.

Chapter Six
The Second Meeting

Donald and Marlene met again in September as they had arranged. Marlene packed a picnic of home-made veal and ham pie with tiny late season tomatoes and slices of a spicy raisin cake that had been an especial favourite of her father's. Donald ate every last crumb as if he was starving and Marlene could see that she was making progress with her cooking. She asked Donald several questions about his cottage that Donald seemed rather reluctant to answer. Finally, she decided to be frank with him.

'I enjoy your company Donald, and I have looked forward to our meeting today but before we can go any farther down the road that we are both thinking of I will have to see your cottage and smallholding.'

Donald sighed, knowing that Marlene was unlikely to be impressed with his home, but agreed that she should visit him in October to see it for herself. Marlene suggested that she should catch the coach to Millbrook, and she could stay in the local pub. Donald was aghast at this suggestion and immediately put a stop to any such idea.

'No, no, no,' he said emphatically, 'you'll set every tongue in the place wagging if you turn up like that. You don't realise what a shocking place a village is for gossip.'

Marlene suggested another idea that had occurred to her that she should travel by train to Ludlow, stay overnight at a little bed and breakfast place she knew of with a view of the river and the castle and then Donald could collect her next morning and drive her to his home. They could have a bite of lunch somewhere and Marlene would return to London on the afternoon train.

Donald was much happier with this suggestion. With a bit of luck he could get Marlene in and out without a soul knowing about it. No need to set the tongues wagging any sooner than they had to.

They packed up the picnic and put the basket in the car before taking a stroll around the town, comfortable in each other's company but still discreetly summing each other up, Marlene occasionally having difficulty with Donald's broad west country accent and Donald wondering what it would be like to live with a woman who was so totally unlike anyone he had ever met.

Chapter Seven
A Visit to the Cottage

As the days passed and the time for Marlene's visit drew closer Donald began to panic. He looked again at the cottage through new eyes and saw the shabby furniture, worn rugs and tired paintwork. There wasn't much he could do apart from drag out the old vacuum cleaner and give the place a good clean. He dusted diligently for the first time for many months, washed the kitchen floor, tidied out the pantry and washed out his primitive toilet, although he was secretly hoping that Marlene would not need to look in there.

He was busy cleaning the windows when Tater came to visit, provoking more awkward questions from Tater that he did his best to avoid. Tater had known his cousin all his life and he was absolutely certain that Donald was up to something. He was being so shifty and evasive and talked about an old friend from the army that Tater had never ever heard him mention before. Tater was sure there was a woman involved somewhere but try as he might, and his powers of detection were awesome, he could not find out who the woman was.

Donald shook out the front and back door mats, disturbing earwigs and woodlice that had been comfortably at home for months. He swept all around the house and as a finishing touch picked a bunch of bronze and yellow chrysanthemums from the garden and put them in a vase in the little sitting room. Before he left for Ludlow, he made sure the woodstove was well stoked and that there was plenty of water drawn from the well. He didn't want to call attention to it by having to go out and pump while Marlene was there. He glanced around before he shut the door. To him the old place looked homely and comfortable, and he just hoped Marlene would look at it the same way. He was glad the sun was shining for even if it did show up the worn patches it made everything more cheerful than a gloomy overcast day. He began to realise how dreary his home life had become and how much he was hoping that Marlene would become his wife. He was surprised at the strength of his feelings, not necessarily for Marlene herself but for what she could bring into his life.

He dressed carefully, locked up the cottage and took a back road to Ludlow that avoided the centre of the village, arriving at the bed and breakfast just after 10 am Marlene was waiting for him and greeted him happily, eager to be gone and to see his cottage at last.

The countryside was looking beautiful in the late autumn sunshine, the trees still in their autumn colours and Marlene enjoyed the drive through the winding country lanes, through quaint black and white villages and rich farming land where the famous red and white Hereford cattle grazed peacefully. Donald was silent for most of the journey, concentrating on his driving and anxious about Marlene's reaction to the cottage. He was worrying needlessly for Marlene was entranced with what she saw.

For the first time for many years Donald entered the house through the front door, showing Marlene into the parlour, where a fire glowed in the grate and the chrysanthemums gave the room a welcoming look. Marlene looked around, taking in the need for painting and refurbishing but also seeing the possibilities of the room. It was a comfortable size, warm and homely, she liked what she saw. They passed through to the old-fashioned dining room, furnished with heavy dark furniture with deep red curtains at the windows. It was a room that had seldom been used even when Donald's parents were alive.

Up the narrow staircase were two bedrooms, a good-sized double room, a single room and a tiny box room, all in need of a good coat of paint and new curtains and rugs but nothing that Marlene felt she could not tackle.

It was not until they came to the kitchen and scullery area that Marlene began to have misgivings about what she might be letting herself in for. She eyed the tap-less stone sink and the woodstove doubtfully.

'What about water?' she asked in a quiet voice.

'I draws it from the well outside,' said Donald. ''Tis beautiful clean water, none of those chemicals in it that you get in the town water.'

'Where do you wash and bathe?' asked Marlene. 'Where's the toilet?'

'I washes at the sink here,' said Donald. 'When I want a bath, I fill the copper and light a fire under it and puts the hot water in that zinc tub in front of the woodstove here. There's nothing nicer than sitting in here having a good hot bath,' he said hopefully.

'And the toilet?' asked Marlene faintly.

'Out here,' said Donald taking Marlene out the back door and a short distance along the path to where the little outhouse stood. Donald opened the door he had hoped would remain firmly shut during Marlene's visit. Marlene viewed the primitive bucket toilet with its old-fashioned wooden seat and squares of newspaper for toilet paper with distaste.

'It's all right for you to wrinkle your nose, my dear, but there's nothing like that for getting the rhubarb to grow!' Donald said, somewhat nettled by Marlene's reaction. Marlene had never lived anywhere that did not have hot and cold running water, a bathroom and a flush toilet, except during the war years when her father had evacuated his wife and little daughter to a cottage in the depths of the Devonshire moors. Marlene's mother had survived for eighteen months with no electricity and running water in the safety of the remote village before returning to civilisation and air raids.

Marlene pulled out a chair and sat herself at the kitchen table.

'Make a cup of tea and let's have a talk about this,' she said.

Donald pulled the kettle on to the hotplate of the woodstove and set cups and saucers out on the table. He fetched a tin of biscuits from the pantry and brewed the tea. Marlene sighed.

'This is a lovely place you have here, Donald,' she said 'but you can't really expect a woman to live like this in this day and age. I've got my own little fridge and an electric stove that would fit in that corner over there, I can bring a good three-piece suite and a double and single bed and between us we could make this very comfortable. But there is no way I could consider living here without water being laid on to the house.'

Donald sipped his tea and looked at her narrowly.

'Before we go any further,' he said, 'you must be honest with me. Are you seeing any other fellows besides me? You must have had other replies to your advertisement in the paper. You see, I'm not going to go to the expense of bringing water to the house, only to have you go off and wed someone else.'

Donald didn't like to say that was what had happened with the electricity, but he wasn't going to get caught twice.

'Don't misunderstand me, my dear, if you are serious about coming to live here, I will look into it, but for myself I am more than happy with things as they are, and it would be foolish of me to spend my hard earned money on something I don't need.'

Marlene flushed. This was the closest they had come to admitting that they were considering marriage and she thought hard before committing herself.

'I'm not seeing anyone else, Donald. I like you and I like your cottage and, yes, I will consider coming to live here with you if you have the water laid on.'

Donald smiled. 'That's settled then, come and have a look around the garden,' he said happily.

Little did Marlene realise that those few words 'have the water laid on' would be the cause of an ongoing feud between them for many months to come.

They strolled around the garden in the late autumn sunshine looking at the neat vegetable garden, the large henrun where a motley collection of hens were dusting themselves in the sun and the fields where Donald kept bullocks to fatten for the market. It was while they were leaning over the gate looking at the bullocks that Tater pedalled around the side of the cottage, propped his old bike against the shed and came sauntering over to join them.

'Well then, Donald, are you going to introduce me to your old army friend from London?' He winked in Marlene's direction, holding out a weather-worn brown hand.

'I'm Donald's cousin, Hugh,' he said shaking her hand. 'Donald's been keeping very quiet about you, you know, but I guessed there was something in the wind the way he's been sprucing the old place up of late.'

Donald glared at Tater. 'Was there anything special you were wanting?' he asked.

'Nothing really,' said Tater cheerfully. 'I know when I'm not wanted. I only looked in for a chat, but as you are busy, I will be on my way.'

He pedalled off up the lane with every last detail of Marlene's appearance stored in his memory, leaving Donald annoyed by the interruption.

'It will be all over the village by nightfall that you've been here,' he said. 'I was hoping to keep it quiet.'

It was time for them to make the return journey to Ludlow if they were to have lunch before Marlene caught her train back to town. Marlene took one last look at the cottage before they drove away. She would not see it again until she was Mrs Donald Evans.

When Marlene parted from Donald at Ludlow station, she invited him to visit her at her little flat for Christmas dinner and Donald agreed to come.

Chapter Eight
Christmas Celebrations

Marlene went to a lot of trouble to decorate her little flat, buying a tiny Christmas tree and hanging up some of the old paper chains that hadn't seen the light of day for many years. She planned a special meal of smoked salmon mousse, followed by roasted chicken with bacon rolls, stuffing and roast potatoes, parsnips, brussels sprouts and peas with gravy, followed by Christmas pudding with custard and brandy sauce and mince pies. Her Uncle Tom, Auntie Glad and Cousin Sheila, or Sossie as she was known in the family, were to come on Boxing Day so the extra food would not go amiss. Marlene baked a rich fruit cake and iced it decorating it with little fir trees and Father Christmas with his sack of toys.

Both Marlene and Donald gave a considerable amount of thought as to what they should give each other for Christmas gifts. Marlene finally settled upon a new shirt and tie and a pair of socks for Donald, not that she was hinting at anything, but it had become plain after their meetings that he had only one halfway respectable shirt and tie, and she could swear that he had worn the same pair of socks each time, too.

Donald pondered over the problem of his gift for hours for he had no experience of buying gifts for a woman. He finally hunted out his mother's inlaid wooden box in which she had kept all her trinkets. He laid them out on the table and looked them over. They were mostly worthless bits and pieces that she had won at the May Fair, for in her day his mother had been a dab hand at the skittles and the sideshows, never failing to come home with her arms full of trophies. In amongst the tawdry fairground rubbish there was a marcasite bow brooch that his father had given to his mother on their wedding day and a little gold brooch that Donald thought had belonged to his grandmother. He finally settled on the marcasite brooch and put it to one side, replacing all the other items in the box which he stowed away once again in the chest of drawers in the bedroom.

Donald washed the brooch carefully in hot soapy water and dried it and packed it in a wisp of tissue paper that had been kept by for just such a purpose for many years. Nothing was ever wasted in his house.

Donald then went to the cupboard under the stairs and sorted out a bottle of parsnip wine that he had made four years ago and which he considered to be some of the best wine he had ever made. He found a bottle of plum brandy and agonised over whether he should take it. He wouldn't be able to drink much if he was going to turn around and drive home again and it might look bad to pick it up and take it away once he had given it to Marlene, but then again if they were to wed, she would never have drunk it all by the time they were married and he would get it back again anyway! He decided to take it as he didn't want to look mean and risk losing Marlene.

On Christmas Day Donald was up early, tended to the poultry and stock and was ready to leave by 9 am. He changed into his sports jacket and corduroy trousers, pulled the back door to, jumped into the old pick-up and was on his way before Tater or anyone else could come around to wish him a Happy Christmas and drink his wine. He had a good journey and arrived in Watford in just over three hours. He could smell the chicken roasting as he stood on the doorstep of Marlene's little flat and rang the bell. She opened the door to greet him wearing a new red dress with a flowered apron over it.

'Happy Christmas, Donald,' she cried, 'come in and get warm.' She took his coat from him.

'Happy Christmas, Marlene.' Donald bent towards her and gave her a light peck on the cheek. They both blushed and Marlene busied herself hanging up Donald's coat while Donald put the wine on the sideboard in the little living room.

'The dinner is just about ready to dish up, so you've timed it nicely,' said Marlene as she came back into the room. 'It is a long way for you to drive in one day.'

'T'is worth it to see you, m'dear,' said Donald gallantly. 'I've brought you a little gift.' He handed her the tiny tissue wrapped parcel. 'T'was my dear old mother's brooch but I thought you might like it.'

Indeed Marlene did like it and said so. She then presented Donald with his parcel rather shyly as she hoped it would not cause offence.

'I didn't know what to get you,' she said, 'but I couldn't help noticing that a new shirt wouldn't come amiss.'

Donald was speechless. No one had ever given him such a present in his life and Marlene's extravagance alarmed him. It was all very good and useful clothing no doubt, and Marks and Spencer were reasonably priced, but to buy so much! Ah well, if they didn't end up getting married it would compensate him for all the money spent on petrol and postage stamps.

'Thank you very much, m'dear, 'tis just what I've been wanting,' he said carefully rewrapping the parcel ready to take home with him.

They sat down to enjoy their meal, toasting each other in parsnip wine which was a deceptively innocent wine with a powerful alcoholic content. They feasted magnificently, finishing their meal with the Christmas pudding ablaze with brandy. Donald had not eaten food like it for years and doubted whether his dear old mother had produced a better meal.

After they had eaten, Donald and Marlene sat in the little living room, sipping plum brandy and nibbling on mince pies as they planned their wedding. Marlene had set her heart on having a church wedding but when she mentioned having the banns called three weeks before the wedding Donald balked. There was no way he was going to tell the whole village that he was getting married in three weeks' time. Give them that long and they would have a whole busload turning up looking for free food and drink. Donald was all for a quiet little affair in the local Registry Office.

'How many people do you expect to come from your side then, Donald?' asked Marlene.

'Just me and Tater,' said Donald. 'No need for anyone else as far as I can see. How about you?'

'Well, Uncle Tom and Auntie Glad, and my cousin Sossie,' said Marlene. 'I was planning to ask some of the people I work with, too, but if that is all you are having let's keep it small.'

'What sort of a name is Sossie for goodness's sake?' Donald asked. 'Is it a boy or a girl?'

'Sossie is my cousin Sheila,' said Marlene. 'She is about the same age as me and has been called Sossie all her life because she is shaped just like a sausage. You'll see what I mean when you meet her. She lives in

Bournemouth with Uncle Tom and Auntie Glad and works as a librarian.'

'Have you told her about me yet?' asked Donald.

'No,' Marlene admitted. 'I haven't told anyone. They are all coming here for a meal tomorrow so I will tell them then. There will be a bit of an uproar when I tell them I expect but it's nobody's business except ours.' She tossed her head defiantly pretending she didn't care. 'We are old enough to know what we are doing after all,' she said trying to sound convincing.

Donald nodded off in front of the electric heater and Marlene crept out to clear up and wash the dishes while he slept. When she had finished, she set a tray with tea cups and slices of her Christmas cake, brewed the tea and carried it into the living room. She stood looking down at this strange man whom she had agreed to marry in just two months' time. How much did she really know about him? How could she find out apart from hiring a private detective to dig into his background? She would just have to trust her instincts. He seemed a decent enough person to her and surely life in a country cottage with a companion would be preferable to the sterile existence of her present way of life.

Donald stirred and awoke to find Marlene studying him intently. Had he been talking in his sleep? Had he been snoring? Oh dear! Who was this strange woman he was planning to marry? He stifled his doubts, stood up and stretched.

'Ah,' he said. 'There is just time for a nice cup of tea and some of that lovely cake, and then I must be away again.'

'I'll wrap up a piece of the cake for you to take home with you,' said Marlene. 'It will take me weeks to eat it all on my own.'

Donald gathered his things about him, and Marlene handed him a parcel of cake, pudding and mince pies.

'That's settled then,' said Marlene, 'we'll get married on the first Saturday in March in the Watford Registry Office. I'll let you know all the details about time and everything when I've made some enquiries.'

They gave each other another bashful kiss and Donald thanked Marlene for the delicious meal before getting back into the old pick-up to drive home. Marlene watched until he was out of sight before returning to the little flat shaking up cushions and tidying up before she put on her coat and went for a brisk walk. Whatever were Uncle Tom and Auntie Glad going to say tomorrow when they heard that she was getting married? Oh well, she'd cross that bridge when she reached it. No point in worrying now.

Chapter Nine
The Wedding

The morning of their wedding day dawned overcast and grey with a thick drizzly mist reducing visibility. The ceremony was planned for eleven o'clock after which they would adjourn to a nearby pub where Marlene had booked a private room and arranged for a meal to be served. Marlene, who had spent the last week living with her neighbour while she cleaned up her flat and packed her furniture ready for storage, was doggedly going ahead with her plans to marry Donald in the face of some very stiff opposition from her family and friends, all of whom counselled her to think again and not to commit herself to the marriage.

Marlene had shopped for her wedding outfit in Oxford Street, agonising over a lovely dress with a matching loose coat in a soft rose-pink wool. However, when she cast her mind over the cottage, and the accommodation that was waiting for her after her marriage, she put the outfit to one side and settled instead for a more practical suit in a soft cocoa brown and a head hugging hat with a little pink rose under the brim. With a pair of low-heeled court shoes and matching gloves and bag she felt it was a suitable outfit for the occasion.

Before changing into her wedding outfit Marlene walked to the local florists to collect her spray of pink roses, lilies of the valley and gardenias and the corsages and buttonhole for Uncle Tom, Auntie Glad and Sossie. Marlene had invited Mrs Wright, with whom she had been staying and two of her friends from work to come to the wedding reckoning that as Uncle Tom had offered to pay for the meal it was not going to cost Donald anything if she had extra guests.

At 10.30 am Uncle Tom arrived in a taxi to take Marlene and Mrs Wright to the registry office, having already left Auntie Glad and Sossie there. A small group of residents from the flats where Marlene had lived for so many years gathered to wish her well and wave her away and Marlene was surprised to find that she had tears in her eyes as she left. Perhaps her old life hadn't been so bad after all!

A stickler for punctuality, Uncle Tom had the bride ready and waiting at the registry office a quarter of an hour before the appointed time and they shivered in the chilly March air as they waited for Donald to arrive.

The time ticked past, and the little group moved into the warmth of the registry office while they waited. 11 o 'clock came and went, five past, ten past, a quarter past and no sign of the groom and his best man. At twenty past eleven Marlene and Uncle Tom were standing on the doorstep of the building as the mist swirled around them. The Registrar was becoming anxious and fidgety for another marriage had been booked for 11.45. Suddenly, the old red pick-up appeared out of the mist with Tater waving and gesticulating from the passenger seat before it disappeared again, and five minutes later Donald and Tater arrived, breathless and damp, muttering about being unable to find a hill to park on. Uncle Tom hustled them unceremoniously into the room where the Registrar was waiting, and the marriage was finalised at top speed as the guests for the next wedding started to make their appearance.

When the moment came for Donald to slip the wedding ring on Marlene's finger, she found herself wearing a thin, worn ring several sizes too large.

'T'was my dear old mother's ring, m' dear,' Donald murmured as if he was bestowing a priceless treasure upon her.

A few quick photographs taken on the steps of the Registry Office and the bride and groom, and guests adjourned to the nearby public house for a much needed drink and warm up by the open fire. Uncle Tom buttonholed Donald almost immediately demanding an explanation for his lateness and Donald explained that the battery on his pick-up was flat and the car wouldn't start without a push. He had spent the best part of half an hour looking for a hill on which he could park so that he could roll the car downhill and start it on the way home. If need be, Tater could give it a bit of a push.

'Why ever didn't you buy a new battery, man if you knew it was as flat as that?' Uncle Tom demanded. 'After all it is your wedding day.'

Donald blinked through his glasses in surprise. 'Well for one thing I thought a good run to London would charge it up a bit,' he said, 'and there's still a bit of life in it yet. You can't go throwing good money away on things like that before it's necessary, can you?'

Uncle Tom gave up in disgust and took himself off to get warm by the fire. Goodness knows what Marlene had done getting herself involved with this fellow. He'd warned her sternly enough, but she had been determined to go through with it. Uncle Tom looked dourly across at Donald, noting with distaste that his suit didn't quite fit him and had probably been made for a slightly shorter, fatter man. It had in fact belonged to Donald's father who had a good ten years of wear out of the suit before he died.

The mood of the party lifted after they had eaten a good meal and toasted the newlyweds with a glass of champagne. Uncle Tom wished them 'The best of British luck' and then it was time for Donald and Marlene to be on their way. Donald rounded up Tater from the corner of the room where he had been getting quietly drunk with a bottle of whisky that he had cadged from the bar and put down to Uncle Tom's account. Marlene kissed her family and friend's goodbye, there was a sprinkling of confetti, Donald picked up her new suitcase and Marlene carried the wedding gifts as they left to walk to where the pick-up had been parked.

It soon became painfully obvious that Tater was in no state to walk and Marlene was left to carry her suitcase as well as the gifts as Donald supported his inebriated cousin, and they hurried along as well as they could in the thick misty rain. Once they reached the car Donald tossed Marlene's case in the back, covering it with a scrap of tarpaulin and thrust the semiconscious Tater into the front seat.

'You push from behind and I'll run alongside here, and we'll soon be away,' he said.

Marlene, her temper rising by the moment, pushed as she was told, the car rolled down the hill and the engine fired just as they approached a large roundabout. Donald leapt into the driving seat, revved up the engine and drove away, leaving Marlene, wet and furious in the middle of the road. Donald circled the roundabout, pulled up beside her and urged her to hurry up and get in as he was holding up the traffic. Marlene clambered over Tater's prostrate body and found herself squashed against Donald. Using her nails and heels she forced Tater into the corner to give herself more room. 'I suppose he'll be coming on honeymoon with us too!' she spat furiously.

'Oh no, m'dear, we'll be dropping him off at his cottage on the way through the village,' Donald reassured her, patting her knee in a way that reminded her of her meeting with Reg.

Marlene made herself as small as she could, not deigning to touch either of the men with whom she was sharing the cab and sat in silence until they pulled up outside Tater's cottage where Donald deposited him untidily on his bed to sober up.

'Where are we going to now, then?' asked Marlene as they pulled out of the village and headed west.

'We're going to Wales for a day or two to a little place I know of,' said Donald. 'Just you sit back and enjoy the drive and we'll soon be there.'

Donald had not been intending to have a honeymoon, but it became plain that Marlene was expecting one. He had found a bargain offer in a Welsh newspaper which he had picked up from The Larches and had made a reservation.

The day darkened into night and the windscreen wipers worked monotonously against the relentless rain. Apart from one stop to change a flat tyre in the middle of the Welsh hills it was an uneventful journey. At last they pulled up outside a little private hotel in Aberystwyth. Marlene was about to ask how long they would be staying when a sign caught her eye. 'OFF SEASON SPECIAL' it announced, 'TWO NIGHTS FOR THE PRICE OF ONE.' She had been married to

Donald for less than a day, but she already knew the answer to her question.

Marlene left Donald at the desk signing the register and followed a porter to their room.

'Your husband will be up in a moment, madam,' he said politely, guessing that Marlene was newly married as she still had confetti clinging to her hair.

'Who?' asked Marlene and then blushed as she realised her mistake. 'Oh yes, of course,' and the porter grinned to himself as he went back downstairs.

Marlene took off her damp jacket and slipped into a cardigan while she waited for Donald. She was starving hungry and dying for a cup of tea or a drink as she had been too overwrought to eat much after the wedding and it had been a long drive. Donald came into the room rubbing his hands and headed to the heater to warm himself up.

'Let's get ourselves tidied up and then go and find a meal,' said Marlene, 'I'm starving.'

'Oh, don't let's be too hasty,' said Donald. 'I've a nice bit of neck of mutton and some onions and taters in that box there and I've brought the primus along. I can't wait to taste some more of your lovely home cooking, m'dear, so I thought you could make me a nice Irish stew.'

Marlene stared at him in disbelief.

'You expect me to cook Irish stew in here, now?' she said glaring at him ominously, her temper rising for the second time that day. 'For one thing it would take hours and hours, for another it would stink the place out, and for a third thing I am NOT COOKING IRISH STEW ON MY WEDDING NIGHT!'

With that outburst, she threw on her mackintosh, picked up her handbag and stormed out of the room to find a meal, leaving Donald bewildered at the temperamental ways of women.

When Marlene returned to the hotel after having a meal of fish and chips and a hot cup of tea she found Donald already in bed and asleep. She undressed quietly in the bathroom and slipped into the bed alongside him, careful not to touch or disturb him and fell asleep almost instantly after her long and emotional day. She would sort it all out tomorrow she decided as there was nothing she could do now.

Chapter Ten
Wedded Bliss

Donald and Marlene spent the next day exploring Aberystwyth, and on the following morning they packed their bags and headed back to Millbrook to begin their married life together in the Stone House. The weather had improved and with it Marlene's temper although relations between the pair were still as frosty as the chilly and fresh March air.

Marlene had been talking about how she was looking forward to seeing the new plumbing in the cottage, asking Donald questions about the new bathroom that he had had to dodge and he knew before they entered the cottage that there was another first class row on the horizon.

Donald was relieved that Tater was nowhere to be seen when they arrived at the cottage and thought disgustedly that his cousin was probably still sobering up. He opened the back door and stood back for Marlene to go in. It didn't occur to him that at least he should have taken his new bride in the front door, even if he didn't carry her over the threshold.

Marlene put her bag on the kitchen table, took off her hat and had a long look around. She walked over to the stone kitchen sink, now sporting a cold tap and a wooden handle similar to those used to pull beer in the pubs.

'What is this for?' she asked. 'I've never seen one of these before.'

Donald was eager to demonstrate.

'This is how I've laid the water on my dear,' he said, pumping away at the handle. 'You pumps here backwards and forwards like this, and the water comes up from the well and goes into that tank over the stairs there, like, and then when you turns on the tap you have water at the sink.'

Donald was proud of his effort, which had cost him very little. The tank had been up against the shed for a year or two and had been used occasionally by the fowls, but he had given it a good wash out and it was as good as new. He had picked up some pipe at a sale and had only to buy the pump handle and the tap.

'What about the bathroom and the toilet, then?' Marlene asked quietly.

'What about them?' asked Donald. 'You have your bath here in the kitchen before the fire every Friday or Saturday night. Why go to all the expense of putting in a bathroom when you only use it once a week at the most?'

'And the toilet?' asked Marlene even more quietly.

'There's nothing wrong with the toilet as it is,' said Donald stoutly. 'I hardly uses it myself, just the once first thing in the morning. When I wants a pee, I do it in the compost heap, does it a power of good.'

He suddenly caught sight of Marlene's face with her eyes and mouth wide open.

'No, no, my dear, I don't expect you to use the compost heap when you want to, ah, relieve yourself. T'wouldn't be any good at all. 'Tis only male urine that is good for it, believe me. What I am trying to say is that you will have your own private toilet except for my one visit first thing. I'll do all the emptying so why go to all the expense of putting in one of those fancy flushing jobs?'

Marlene put on her hat and picked up her bag. 'What time does the next Black and White coach go through?' she asked in despair.

'Now don't you do anything hasty like leaving before we've even started,' cried Donald. 'Just you make yourself at home while I go and take a look around to see that everything's been alright while I've been away. T'would be foolish to give up so soon after all the trouble and expense we've been to get ourselves wed, wouldn't it now?' Donald could see that he had put his foot in it again as Marlene's face darkened even more.

'You must be the only man in England who has managed to get married without buying anyone a drink or paying for anything,' she said bitterly.

'But look at all the cost of petrol and two nights in a hotel.' Donald beat a hasty retreat. 'Just you make yourself comfortable, like I said, while I take a look around outside.'

He picked up the egg basket and hurried out the back door, too quickly for Tater who had been happily eavesdropping on the quarrelling couple.

'That's what you call wedded bliss is it?' called Tater, as he hastily pedalled away on his bike. 'I'll come back later when the pair o' you 'as settled in.'

'Clear off,' growled Donald grumpily.

Marlene sighed as she looked around the bare and shabby kitchen. She had only herself to blame. She had enough warnings from Uncle Tom and Auntie Glad and the girls at work. If she went back now without even giving the marriage a chance she would be deafened by the chorus of 'I told you so!' from every one of them. There was no way she was going to give them that satisfaction so she would just have to make the best of it.

Chapter Eleven
Housekeeping

Marlene despondently took off her outdoor things and put them away in the double bedroom. She had intended to make the single room hers but for some reason Donald had removed the old flock mattress and taken it out to the barn to make a warm pen for a sick calf. All that remained on the single bed were the springs. She hunted through her suitcase for her apron and went into the kitchen where she retrieved Donald's ingredients for an Irish stew from the box he had put on the table and set about making a meal for both of them. She put it on the top of the stove ready for when Donald should come back in and light the fire. She was blowed if she was going to do that. If she was staying she would have her little electric stove and her fridge sent down from London as soon as she could.

While she was waiting for Donald to return Marlene made a thorough check of the kitchen and pantry and found little to cheer her up. She could have her pots and pans and utensils sent down too but it would take a major shopping expedition to stock the pantry, which contained little apart from some baked beans and sardines, a packet of tea and a few biscuits.

Donald came back into the kitchen bringing the cold air with him. He put a basket of eggs in the pantry and fetched some morning wood to light the stove. Marlene began to get a glimmer of what she was up against when she saw Donald open his pocket knife and painstakingly split a match in half before he lit the fire, carefully putting the unused half back in the matchbox.

With the woodstove going they boiled a kettle and put the stew on to simmer. Donald brewed the tea and put out the rather stale biscuits. Neither of them spoke as they sat at the kitchen table sipping their tea. Then Marlene said, 'I've decided to stay for a week or so to see if we can work things out. I'm sorry if you feel I'm unreasonable about the bathroom but I thought you understood what I meant. I realise now I should have come again to see what you had done before we went ahead with the wedding.'

She paused and sipped her tea and Donald eyed her thoughtfully. She might look all meek and demure but by golly there was a fiery woman underneath that mild exterior. He was going to have to play his cards very carefully if he wanted to get his own way with her.

'We'll have to go shopping to get some food in either this afternoon or first thing in the morning,' said Marlene. 'I can't do much with what is in the pantry.'

'How much money would you be thinking of spending, then?' asked Donald anxiously. 'I'm a bit short as it is with all the expense of the honeymoon.'

Marlene sighed. She thought of a figure and hastily added ten pounds on to it as she realised Donald would certainly quarrel with any amount she suggested.

'I should think about thirty-five pounds would do for a start,' she said, smiling to herself as she saw the consternation on his face.

'Thirty-five pounds! Why that would feed an army for a month!' he complained. 'Ten pounds should be ample, it will fill the pantry to overflowing.'

'Make it twenty pounds then,' said Marlene, 'and I'll do my best with that.'

Donald was reluctant to push the point any harder as he still felt that Marlene was on the brink of rushing back to London.

'While we are on the subject of money, how much housekeeping do you expect me to manage on each week?' Marlene asked. She might as well know the worst at the outset before she settled in.

'Well.' Donald was hesitant. 'I had in mind three pound ten shillings.' He saw Marlene's face beginning to cloud again. 'Just a moment before you dive in the deep end again,' he said hastily, 'take into account that I am going to give you the job of looking after the poultry and you will make yourself anything up to five pounds a week out of eggs and dressed birds. I'll kill them for you but I'll show you how to dress them properly and they sell for a good price in the market, and people are always after the eggs.' Somehow he managed to make his offer sound generous. Then he spoilt the effect by adding, 'Of course, if you are going to bring in your new-fangled electric stove and a refrigerator I shall expect you to pay for the electric too. The meter is behind the door in the pantry and it takes two shilling pieces.'

Marlene looked at Donald in disbelief.

'You expect me to feed us both, clothe myself and pay the electricity bill on three pounds ten a week. I'm not a magician, man, and I am not going to live in poverty. I was earning twelve pounds a week in my job and had it all to spend on myself.'

'Well, you should have stayed in your job, my dear, shouldn't you. You're living in the depths of the country now and people around these parts think they are well off if they can get ten pound a week for a full week's work. I'll tell you what, if you will give me a hand in the garden too I'll let you sell the surplus vegetables as well as the eggs. I can dig over a bit more land and make the vegetable patch larger.'

Marlene sighed. 'Make it five pounds a week and I'll give it a go,' she said reluctantly.

Donald smiled. 'Right you are then. Five pound a week, all the proceeds from the poultry and any extra vegetables we manage to produce. I think that's fair enough. Maybe I could get a cow and you could milk it and make farmhouse butter. That sells well too.'

'Wait a bit before you do that,' said Marlene. 'I'll have enough on my plate learning how to look after the hens and the garden first.'

Chapter Twelve
Village Gossip

As the days passed Donald and Marlene began to settle into a routine. With patient coaching from Donald Marlene gradually mastered the art of cooking on a wood stove and began to produce some delicious and wholesome meals. She was a quick learner and found country life, so different from her days spent travelling to and fro to the heart of London, very much to her liking, She kept this fact to herself, keeping Donald on tenterhooks in case she decided to return to London and her old life. Donald was treading very carefully, biting his tongue rather than complain about any extravagance on Marlene's part for he was more than happy with her cooking skills and her aptitude in the garden.

Marlene solved the problem of her daily wash by waiting until Donald was in the kitchen, then fetching a can of warm water and using the old fashioned wash stand in the bedroom. She had her first experience of taking a bath in the zinc tub by the woodstove in the kitchen when Friday night came around. Donald made all the preparations, heated the water in the old copper and stoked up the fire so that the kitchen was cosily warm. Marlene took her own precautions against any unwanted interruption in the form of the ever-inquisitive Tater turning up at an inopportune moment by locking the back door and pegging the curtains close against any prying eyes. As a final touch she stood the old wooden clothes airer around the tub and draped it with towels. Once she was satisfied that she had done everything possible to ensure her privacy Marlene took off her pink woollen dressing gown and stepped into the hot water, made fragrant with the scent of her violet bath salts. After she had luxuriated in the warmth and given herself a thorough wash she stepped out, dried herself, put on her nightgown and dressing gown and went to join Donald in the living room.

Donald stood up and stretched.

'Righto, my turn now then,' he said as he went in to the kitchen. 'Great heavens woman! What have you put in the water then?' he shouted. 'It smells like a florist's shop out here! I can't bathe in that!'

Marlene went into the kitchen looking perplexed. 'You don't intend to use the same water as me do you?' she asked.

'Of course I do,' said Donald. 'It's good hot water and it isn't as if you are dirty. You wash every day. It'll have to do I suppose,' he said grumpily, 'but don't you go putting any of that there smelly stuff in my bath again. It won't do the plants any good either. I uses the bath water in the garden and the greenhouse, tis good for the greenfly and those sorts of things.'

Marlene returned to the living room feeling chastened. She had never thought of her bath as extravagant before. It had never occurred to her to save or re-use her bathwater or to refrain from using bath salts so that her plants could benefit. Life was certainly different in the country.

It took Marlene a day or two to pluck up enough courage to go into the village as she was only too well aware that she was the subject of much gossip amongst the villagers. The time came, however, when she could no longer put the visit off as there were several dozen eggs to be taken to the shop and one or two items which she needed for the kitchen. She wrapped herself up against the blustery March wind, pulled the door to, picked up her basket of eggs and set off. Marlene was not in a very happy mood, having had to put up with yet another of Tater's visits and listen to him making his malicious comments about lovebirds and newlyweds. She knew that there was one person who would be only too happy to see her marriage fail and witness the sight of her leaving for London.

Mary Goodings was serving old Joan Wainwright when Marlene entered the shop and both women turned to give her a long inquisitive stare. They both knew immediately who she must be and were full of curiosity about this stranger from London who had managed to marry the meanest man in the district and come and live in their midst without them knowing anything about it.

'Donald sent some eggs for you Mrs Goodings,' said Marlene putting the basket on the counter, 'and I'll take some self-raising flour and a packet of bicarbonate of soda thank you.'

Mary Goodings put the flour and baking soda on the counter and counted out the money for the eggs. Marlene was just turning to go when Joan Wainwright spoke.

'However did you come to marry that mean old blighter Donald Evans, then?' she asked. 'He's been looking for a wife ever since his old mother died but no woman for miles around here would look at him, the tight-fisted old bugger.'

Marlene drew herself up to her full height and glared coldly at Mrs Wainwright.

'When I want your opinion on my husband I'll come and ask you for it,' she said, 'and until then I'll thank you to keep your long nose out of my affairs!'

With that she turned and left the shop, slamming the door behind her and setting the little bell tinkling wildly. She walked back to the cottage with her feathers still ruffled, wishing she was back in her little flat with her boring old job.

Marlene was lifting a casserole out of the oven when Donald came in the door for his dinner. He stood watching her for a moment, savouring the warmth of the kitchen and the prospect of a good meal ready for him.

'I hear you've been upsetting the village busybodies,' he said, 'telling old Joan Wainwright to mind her own business. Not before time, either, that woman's a proper old cat and causes no end of trouble in the village.'

'I only saw her less than an hour ago,' said Marlene, 'how can you possibly know anything about it?'

'News travels fast in Millbrook, m'dear,' said Donald settling down happily to his plate of stew and dumplings.

Chapter Thirteen
An Unexpected Find

One day the cold east wind, which had been blasting the countryside for nearly three weeks, stopped blowing, the sun came out and spring arrived. Marlene was enchanted with the beauty of the countryside, she delighted in hearing the blackbird's song from the roof of the cottage and in seeing the cows, sheep and hens, relax and luxuriate in the warmth of the spring weather after spending the last few weeks huddling together in miserable groups trying to keep warm.

The same sunshine that brought such magic outside penetrated deeply into the cottage and showed up the shabby furnishings and stained paintwork with unmerciful clarity. After Donald had left to go to the market one Thursday morning Marlene went from room to room in the cottage with a pad and pencil in her hand, noting down everything that needed to be done in order to bring the cottage up to what she herself considered to be an acceptable level of comfort. She scrutinised all the curtains and light-fittings, studied the carpets and furniture, noting what was worth retaining and what was past saving. She was only too well aware that every last thing would have to be done on a shoestring and that Donald would quibble over every penny she spent. However, Marlene was beginning to enjoy country life and was finding that being married to Donald was possibly going to be preferable to living on her own in London. She was still keeping her options open and had not yet sent for her furniture from London, biding her time until she was sure she wanted to stay.

Marlene sat down and estimated how much she would need to do a reasonable job on the cottage and came to the conclusion she would just be able to get by on about one hundred and fifty pounds. When Donald came back from the market that evening Marlene had a savoury pot roast simmering and a steamed jam roly poly pudding bubbling gently on the back of the stove. She waited until Donald had eaten his fill and pushed his chair back with a contented 'by gum, m'dear, that was good.' She noticed that Donald was putting on weight and was beginning to look quite sleek and well cared for since she had taken him in hand.

Marlene cleared away the dishes and waited until they were comfortably seated in front of the living room fire before she tackled Donald on the subject of renovating the cottage. She told him how she had been through the cottage, room by room, and explained to him exactly what she wanted to do. 'As I see it,' she said, 'I could do a very reasonable job and turn this little place into a really nice home and I reckon it would only cost about two hundred pounds at the most.'

Donald who was filling his pipe when she spoke choked suddenly and his pipe flew out of his mouth.

'Two hundred pound,' he exclaimed. 'Whatever do you want to spend that amount for? Look now, this cottage was good enough for my old mother, it's good enough for me and there is no way I'm going to spend that sort of money on it. All it needs is a good spring clean and a lick o' paint, maybe, so I don't want to hear any more nonsense like that.'

And that was that. Donald was adamant for to tell the truth he had spent more money since he had met Marlene than he had ever spent before and his carefully hoarded cash was dwindling. Marlene subsided into silence and picked up her knitting, considering her options and wondering yet again whether to stay or go back to London. After an hour or so of stony silence, Donald, who had also been considering the likelihood of Marlene leaving and not wanting to go back to his old bachelor existence said grudgingly, 'There's some paint in the shed you can have if it is any use to you. I'll sort it out in the morning.'

Marlene sniffed, packed away her knitting and took herself off to bed. When Donald showed her the paint next day it proved to be vivid blue, brilliant yellow and shocking pink.

'Why did you pick those colours?' she asked. 'They're awful.'

'Ah well, I got it cheap you see,' said Donald. 'No one else wanted it.'

'I'm not surprised,' said Marlene and went back into the house.

Donald pedalled off to The Limes to put in a day in the garden there for old Mrs Martin, leaving Marlene to wander disconsolately through the house. She had such lovely plans for it but it couldn't be done without money. She stood in the shabby living room looking at the faded picture of the Stag at Bay that hung over the fireplace. She reached up and lifted it down, exclaiming to herself as she saw the original pale green paint behind the picture contrast with the faded khaki on the rest of the wall. Marlene turned the picture around and idly examined the back of it, noticing as she did that the back of the picture had obviously been sealed and resealed several times. She fetched a knife from the kitchen and slid it around the brown paper backing, lifting it gently from the wooden frame. Her eyes widened as she saw that the back of the picture had been covered with paper thin old fashioned white five pound notes, the sort that 'Promised to pay the Bearer on Demand' in beautiful copperplate script. Scarcely breathing she peeled the notes away, all ten of them, and laid them on the armchair. She propped the picture against the wall and lifted down the Laughing Cavalier.

'Let's see what's behind you,' she muttered as once again she got busy with her kitchen knife. The Laughing Cavalier yielded another fifty pounds and a portrait of Queen Victoria that hung in the dingy dining room produced another forty.

'One hundred and forty pounds,' breathed Marlene. 'I can do a lot with that!'

She took the money upstairs and hid it in a pair of stockings in her underwear drawer before returning to reseal the backs of the pictures and replace them on the walls. When Donald came home for his mid-day meal, she questioned him discreetly about how much money his parents had left.

'Well, everything that my dad had went to mother, o' course,' said Donald, 'and then when she died I reckoned she must have got some cash tucked away somewhere because she was always very careful, like, but I searched high and low and never found a penny so goodness knows what she did with it. I doubt if I'll ever find it now, it must have been stitched in her corsets and got thrown out with them, tis all I can think.'

Donald scratched his head before replacing his cap and leaving to go back to his gardening.

Marlene cleared away the dishes with her mind in a turmoil. The money obviously really belonged to Donald but then like the old saying went 'What you don't have you don't miss' and she could do the cottage up a treat with that amount of money. If she bought a big can of white paint she could mix it with the paint in the shed and have pastel pink and blue and yellow and use some of the white for the ceilings. She would have enough money for brushes and a roller and could buy some new material for curtains. If she gave the carpets a good cleaning and got some new lino for the kitchen floor and had her own pieces of furniture brought down from London the old place would be really cosy. Marlene pondered the problem of how to change the money from the old fashioned and very conspicuous five pound notes to modern currency while she collected the eggs from the henhouse and cleaned them ready for sale.

Chapter Fourteen
The Renovations Begin

That night as she lay in bed Marlene wrestled with her conscience as a committed Christian might wrestle with the devil. What had become of her? She had always been a good and dutiful daughter and had grown up to be a decent law-abiding woman. How could she possibly consider filching her husband's rightful inheritance from under his nose? She should hand the money to Donald in the morning, tell him where she had found it and that would be the end of it. Yes! That would be the end of it. He would salt the money away with the rest of his hoard and she would never have another opportunity to renovate the cottage. Marlene tossed and turned coming first to one decision and then to another.

As another day dawned bright and sunny and the sunshine once again streamed into the cottage Marlene made up her mind. After all the money would be spent improving Donald's property, it wasn't as if she was spending it on herself! After Donald had left for work she wrote a letter to her Uncle Tom who worked in a bank in Bournemouth, explaining to him that she had found the money when she had closed up her little flat but had not mentioned it to him in the flurry of her wedding day. Marlene asked Uncle Tom to verify that the money was still worth something and if it was to have it paid into her bank account. She explained that she did not want to do this locally as she found people so nosy and she preferred to keep her affairs private. Uncle Tom asked no questions, banked the money and posted Marlene's bank book back to her in a few days.

With the money safely in her name Marlene laid her plans for the renovation of the cottage. The next time Donald went into Micklebury Marlene went too, visited the local paint and hardware shop and made several purchases, amongst them a very large tin of white paint, some brushes and rollers, sugar soap and turps, sandpaper and wood filler. When Donald queried her extravagance she explained that she had put some of her own money towards the renovations, together with money that she had saved from the sale of the eggs.

While Donald went off on business Marlene called into a shop specialising in carpets and floor coverings and chose a piece of floral patterned lino to replace the cracked and dirty lino which covered the kitchen floor at present. Marlene prudently decided that Donald would certainly not believe that she had saved enough money from the eggs to make such a purchase and arranged for the lino to be delivered the following day when she intended to make a start on the kitchen.

Marlene was up and about early to get her chores done and out of the way. She packed a lunch for Donald and told him she was going to be doing some spring-cleaning. As soon as he left she stripped the curtains from the window, washed them and had them on the line in no time. She dragged all the furniture outside and set about it with some hot water and sugar soap, scrubbing off years of food and grime and left it in the sun to dry. The next job was to pull up the old lino and then set to work with the sugar soap to get the grease and grime off the walls and ceiling. While it was all drying Marlene headed for the shed, opened up her big tin of white paint and Donald's tin of brilliant yellow. With a bit of tipping and stirring and dabbing of paint on an old piece of wood Marlene produced a dainty pale yellow which she thought would look very pretty on the walls. She painted the ceiling first and was greatly encouraged by the contrast between her fresh white paint and the dingy white which she was covering. A quick break for a cup of tea and a bite to eat and Marlene was off around the walls with her roller covering them with her pale yellow paint. The inside of the little window frame didn't take long and was basically in good condition, the shelving in the little pantry and the doors all took a bit of time but with the warmth from the sun and from the woodstove everything began to dry very nicely. Marlene fetched a screwdriver from the shed and fitted the little glass light shade she had found in a second hand shop to cover the naked globe that provided the light at present. She brought in the curtains, ironed them and put them back in the window, intending to make new ones when her sewing machine came from London with the rest of her stuff. She got down on her knees and scrubbed the kitchen floor, leaving it to dry while she polished the table and chairs outside in the sunshine. Marlene then struggled through the house with the roll of lino that had been left outside the front door, undid the string that held it and unrolled it on the floor. She carried in the table and chairs and looked around in amazement. The little kitchen looked so different! Warm, welcoming and delightful. She glanced quickly at the clock; she would have to hurry to get Donald's meal ready before he came home.

When Donald walked into the kitchen the first thing he noticed was the smell of fresh paint. He looked around him at the transformation that had occurred while he had been at work.

'I see you've been busy, m'dear,' he said nodding around him. ''Tis very nice, very nice indeed.'

Marlene, sitting in an exhausted heap opposite him fervently hoped he wasn't going to start asking questions about how much it had cost, but Donald said no more and applied himself with his usual gusto to his meal. Over the next few weeks he watched with incredulity as his house was transformed, saying little but missing nothing and becoming accustomed to seeing his wife looking like a speckled hen with a fine spray of paint on her hair and face. Donald did not question the cost of the renovations to his home, content that it was not costing him any money. Only Uncle Tom, when he met Marlene several months later, asked her where she had found the old five pound notes. After swearing him to strict secrecy Marlene confided what she had done. Uncle Tom thought it was a huge joke and relished the thought that Donald had been diddled so neatly out of his mother's money.

Chapter Fifteen
The Unfortunate Episode
With the Vicar

Marlene had by now taken over full responsibility for the hens. Donald had shown her how to save all her vegetable peelings and edible kitchen waste and put it into an old black enamel saucepan that was kept for the purpose. Donald then filled the pot up with small potatoes each morning and set it on the woodstove to cook while they breakfasted. After breakfast Marlene would mash the potatoes and scraps with handfuls of bran and pollard, tip the resulting mash into a bucket and carry it through the garden and into the little house paddock. Here the hens joined her, rustling around her feet and hurrying with her to the henhouse where Marlene tipped the mash into their trough, checked that they had plenty of water and collected the eggs in her basket. She learned to keep an eye out for the Rhode Island Red rooster who could launch a vicious attack on any unwary visitor to his harem. Donald taught her how to set a broody hen on a clutch of eggs, letting her out to feed morning and night and how to dress a bird ready for the table. Tater had walked in to examine her first effort and had been scathing about the fact that the bird had lost most of its skin but had retained practically all of its quills. It did indeed look a mess and Marlene had roasted it for their own Sunday dinner, but she was a quick learner and could now dress a bird nearly as well as Donald could.

In the garden Donald proved to be a patient teacher and Marlene a quick and keen student. Donald found it hard to believe that anyone could have lived as long as Marlene had without growing anything other than a pot plant. Marlene learned how to sow seeds, hoe and weed, feed with liquid manure made from a noxious brew that Donald kept in a drum by the shed and to savour the delights of fresh new potatoes, tiny new peas, baby carrots and crisp newly picked beans all of which tasted unlike any vegetables she had ever eaten before. Woe betide Marlene if she should ever put the garden tools away in the shed without first cleaning and oiling them. To leave the tools out in the rain incurred the rough side of Donald's tongue and to put down the secateurs and forget about them, leaving them for Donald to find wet and rusting a week later, warranted a long and tedious lecture on the cost of tools, how most of them had belonged to his father and grandfather before him and how it was impossible to buy good tools nowadays.

Marlene had no doubt that she was learning from a person who was steeped in the art of gardening and between them the garden flourished. One fault that Marlene could not seem to correct, and which earned her many sarcastic remarks from Tater, was the fact that no matter how hard she tried she could not plant out her seedlings or sow her seeds in regimentally straight lines. Donald showed her time and again how to use a line to stake out the row but the results were never quite as they should be. She consoled herself by saying that they grew just as well and tasted just as good but she never did master the art of a truly straight line.

It was at this time that an incident occurred that caused Marlene much anguish and heartache until she finally hit on a way of retaliating. Marlene had been getting up at cockcrow to start the day, feeding and tending the poultry, working in the garden, keeping up to date with the housework and washing and ironing, baking bread and cooking as well as spending a day or so each week painting and renovating the house. She was revelling in the hard work and enjoying the new experience of living by the rhythm of the seasons, but in trying so hard and taking on so much she was a little keyed up and liable to fly off the handle.

One morning Marlene was standing at the kitchen sink washing up after baking some scones and a fruit cake and looking idly out of the window as she did so, admiring her newly planted flower bed which she had made near the clothes line. All of a sudden Marlene became aware that the hens had got into the garden and three or four of them were in the process of scratching in her newly turned flower bed, sending her carefully cherished little bedding plants flying as they searched for grubs and worms.

'Drat those hens,' fumed Marlene as she grabbed her broom, yanked open the kitchen door and set off out at full speed, broom at the ready to send the hens flying and teach them a lesson. Unfortunately for Marlene the vicar had just turned the corner of the cottage and was about to knock on the back door He was right in the path of Marlene's charge and down he went with a broom head in the midriff with Marlene sprawled on top of him. Marlene leapt to her feet full of apologies, helped him up and dusted him down, surreptitiously trying to remove some hen manure from his backside. Marlene helped the vicar into the kitchen, sat him on a chair and made him a cup of tea still apologising profusely and explaining what had happened.

Nothing more would have come of the incident if Tater hadn't happened to be standing in the shed talking to Donald and had seen the whole episode from start to finish. Tater was a born mimic with a malicious ability to parody events such as he had just witnessed, and he polished and embroidered the little episode until it became his party piece at the pub. He would borrow an apron and a broom from the publican, charge along the bar cursing the hens and finish by apologising to the vicar in a high falsetto voice. It never failed to earn him a free pint and news of his little pantomime soon percolated back to Marlene on the village grapevine.

Chapter Sixteen
Cousin Vi's Wedding

Donald's cousin Vi, a nurse who lived in the neighbouring village of Rawton, was to get married early in July. Many years before Vi had been engaged to Owen Pryce, a young motor mechanic and they had been saving hard to get married. One night, coming home from work on his motor bike Owen had taken a corner just a little too fast, there had been ice on the road where the sun had not reached it during the day and Owen had come off his bike and been killed.

Since then Vi had thrown herself into her job and had become the local district nurse. She was very popular in Rawton and was getting married to Jeff Powell the local butcher. It promised to be a good wedding. Marlene regarded the forthcoming wedding as something of an ordeal for she would be introduced to Donald's widespread family for the first time. She was well aware that many people in the district regarded her with a great deal of mistrust as they could not understand why she should ever have wanted to marry Donald. Marlene was anxious that they should both make a good impression at the wedding.

The subject of the wedding present was a matter of considerable discussion between them. Marlene was all for buying some sheets or towels, something useful, whereas Donald was loath to part with any money and was all for taking along a couple of bottles of his gooseberry wine which had turned out a little sour and it would be a good way of getting rid of it. They compromised with Marlene buying some embroidered pillowcases out of the egg money and Donald reluctantly putting in a bottle of damson wine.

The morning of the wedding dawned fine and sunny and Donald was away early to do some work for Alf Jenkins at Burbank Farm, intending to be back in good time to get ready for the wedding. Marlene planned to wear her own wedding outfit, which she had looked over and pressed. She had sponged and pressed and done her best with Donald's rather elderly and shiny suit, set out the new shirt and tie and socks which she had bought him for Christmas and polished his best shoes, which like everything else of his had seen better days.

Marlene had water heating on the stove ready for Donald to wash and was standing at the back door looking for him anxiously by the time he finally came pedalling into sight.

'Come on, you're late,' she said as she hustled him into the kitchen, and then gasped. 'Whatever have you been doing? You smell like a pigsty!' she exclaimed in horror.

'Alf Jenkins had me cleaning out the pigs,' said Donald crossly as he shed his working clothes. Marlene hastily dragged the zinc tub into the kitchen and poured in the hot water from the stove.

'Wait there a minute,' she said as she sprinted for the bedroom, returning with her jar of violet bath salts.

'This will kill the smell,' she said hopefully as she sprinkled a lavish amount into the water. She left Donald to bathe and hurried to fetch him a dry towel. There was no time for modesty and after his hasty bath Donald nipped up to the bedroom to dress while Marlene emptied the tub and hung it up outside to dry.

Ready at last, Marlene pinned Donald's home-made buttonhole to his suit and he rushed out to start the car while Marlene put on her hat, picked up the present and turned the key in the backdoor. Try as he might Donald could not get the old pick-up to start for this time not only was the battery flat, but he had forgotten to fill it up with petrol the day before. In desperation he wheeled his old bike out of the shed, snapped his bicycle clips around his ankles and motioned to Marlene to hop on the crossbar.

'With a bit of luck we shall make it to the church before Vi does,' he said grimly as he set off to pedal the two miles to Rawton. Marlene clutched the present with one hand and held on tightly with the other, glad that her hat was a close fitting one that didn't need to be held. Donald pedalled furiously and they arrived at the church just as the bridal party drew up. Donald propped the bike against the stone wall of the churchyard and they crept into the church through the side door just as the organ pealed out to herald the arrival of the bride. Donald was glistening from his exertions on the bike and he fairly hummed with the smell of violets, a fact which set several noses around them twitching and wrinkling.

Too bad, thought Marlene as she stood for the first hymn, better violets than pig manure.

The old church was filled with sunshine and summer flowers and Vi was a radiant bride. The wedding was a happy occasion with a large gathering of family and friends and after the ceremony the cameras clicked. It wasn't until the photographs were developed that anyone noticed that Donald was still wearing his bicycle clips.

The bridal party and the guests walked the few hundred yards from the church to the 'Spotted Bull' where a lavish reception awaited them. Donald, having worked up an almighty thirst with his efforts to get them to the church, took himself quietly off to the bar. There was nothing he enjoyed more than a good feed and free drinks at someone else's expense and he intended to make the most of the opportunity.

Meanwhile Marlene found herself surrounded by an inquisitive group of Donald's female relations. They stood looking at her, summing her up and saying little. Then one elderly great aunt from Birmingham broke the ice. She was a little sparrow of a woman, eighty if she was a day, who was renowned for her plain speaking.

'Whatever possessed you to marry Donald Evans?' she said, asking what they all wanted to know. 'You couldn't find a stingier bugger if you searched the length and breadth of England.'

Marlene drew herself up. She had been waiting for just such a question and had her answer ready. She took a quick look around to make sure Donald wasn't within earshot.

'I married Donald because I think he is a very nice man,' she said sweetly. 'We get along very well together.'

'Well you can see something in him that no one else has managed to find.' The old lady gave her a beady disbelieving stare. 'Good luck to you.'

'How can you live in that dreadful old cottage?' asked Vi's sister Marion.

'It isn't dreadful anymore,' said Marlene. 'All it needed was a good clean and some fresh paint. It's a dear little place.'

Marion raised her eyebrows sceptically.

'I suppose you've got a nice bathroom, and flush toilet, and all mod cons then?' she asked.

'Not yet,' admitted Marlene, 'but I'm working on it. You can't do it all at once.'

The Master of Ceremonies, calling upon them to be seated, saved Marlene from any more embarrassing questions. She felt she had acquitted herself as well as she could and settled down to enjoy the meal and the speeches at Donald's side.

Throughout the afternoon Marlene and most of the older guests drank a very palatable fruit cup. It was a warm day and they all drank several glasses to quench their thirst. They had been assured by Vi herself that it was indeed fruit cup and it had started out as such, but Tater had seen his more sober relations sipping away at it and had laced it with a bottle of vodka when all eyes were on the bride and groom. As a result the usually sober uncles and aunts were flushed and talkative. Auntie Mim gave a saucy rendering of 'My old Man said Follow the Van' twitching her skirts and showing her legs in a way that surprised those who had known her for years as a staid and respectable schoolmistress. Uncle Cecil told Marlene a joke about a stiff cock and a soft pussy that puzzled her for a long time until suddenly the penny dropped and she couldn't stop laughing. Young Dai Powell was violently ill in the car park and fell asleep in a corner, but then he had eaten as much as he could cram in as well as drinking three glasses of the vodka laced fruit cup.

The bride and groom left the reception in a car festooned with toilet paper, covered in shaving cream and towing a motley assortment of tin cans and old boots and soon after the guests began to drift away.

It was late in the afternoon when Donald and Marlene left the reception to return to their cottage. Their minds befogged by drink they trotted unsteadily up and down the line of cars two or three times, looking for the old red pick-up.

'T'aint there,' said Donald blankly.

'No,' said Marlene, swaying slightly as she tried vainly to remember where they had parked the car. Donald groped in his trouser pocket for the car keys and brought out his bicycle clips instead.

'Ah!' he said, looking at them. 'We come on the ol' bike, didn't we girl?'

'We did?' Marlene blinked.

They turned and tottered around to where the bike was still propped against the wall of the churchyard. They had hopped on the bike nimbly enough when they were in a hurry to get to the church, but getting them both back on when they were drunk was quite a different matter. Donald kept saying 'One, two, three, HUP' to Marlene, who gave a little bounce and a hiccup but remained with two feet still on the ground. Donald looked at her crossly. It was one thing for him to get merry but she had no right to get into such a state. He put both arms around Marlene and heaved her up.

'You're like a sack o' taters, girl,' he grumbled, 'what have you been drinking?' he asked as he got a whiff of her vodka laden breath.

'Fruit cup,' Marlene said hiccupping. 'Beeyootiful fruit cup, best I ever tasted,' she crooned. Donald disentangled her arms from around his neck and carefully deposited her on the cross-bar, placed her hands on the handle bars and hastily mounted the bike himself before she had a chance to fall off.

They proceeded to wobble and weave their way along the lane that led to the cottage. They sang as they went *Daisy, Daisy, Give Me your Answer Do* and Marlene kept breaking out into little giggles. She perched on the cross bar, her hat tipped over one eye, holding on with one hand and conducting the singing with the other.

All went well until they came to the last downhill stretch with a sharp right hand bend before they reached the cottage. Then disaster overtook them. The combined weight of the two of them on the old bike was too much for the brakes, which weren't the best anyway, and they sped down the hill rill-tilt-to-Tilbury, far too fast for Donald to be able to take the corner at the bottom. At the last moment Marlene snatched for her hat which blew off in the breeze, the bike lurched and they landed on a pile of hedge trimmings, Marlene first, Donald on top of her and the bike on top of him.

'Phew, you still stink of violets.' Marlene giggled. It was quite a while before they could stop laughing enough to scramble out of the ditch and finish the journey home on foot.

That night for the first time in their marriage they made love, rather inexpertly but to their mutual enjoyment and satisfaction. They were both deeply embarrassed when they awoke, sober, in the morning. They hadn't been able to look each other in the eye for quite a while, but when Marlene thought it over she guessed she might at last have caught a glimpse of what it was that they sang about in all the songs on the radio.

Chapter Seventeen
A Visit to The Doctor

Soon after Vi's wedding a minor but unpleasant health problem that had bothered Marlene since childhood recurred and she knew that she would have to visit a doctor. It was a personal feminine complaint, a bladder infection, and Marlene did not want to discuss it with Donald. She decided to make an appointment to see the doctor on a Tuesday and to travel into Micklebury on the bus while Donald was out at work.

Marlene knew from previous experience that the doctor would require a urine specimen and she hunted for a container to put it in. She was reluctant to use any of her carefully hoarded jam jars as the jam making season was coming into full swing so she hunted in the shed and found an old whisky bottle which Donald had put by. With a bit of contriving she managed to get a reasonable sample into the whisky bottle, wrapped it in newspaper and stood it in the corner of her shopping basket. Marlene then dressed in cool summer clothes and walked up in to the village in time to catch the ten o'clock bus. It was a sultry overcast day with a hint of a thunderstorm in the air. The countryside seemed almost somnolent in the heat, the cows' tails busy swishing off the persistent flies and the sheep seeking the shade of the trees and hedgerows. The cottage gardens were filled with summer blooms and Marlene marvelled at the size of the delphiniums in one garden as she walked past. Maybe she would try growing them next year. Donald wasn't much interested in growing anything that he couldn't eat or sell but there was no reason why she should not have a flower garden. Marlene smiled wryly to herself as she realised that she must be settling down to country life if she was making plans for next year.

Much to her annoyance Tater was waiting at the bus stop when she reached it. In his usual inquisitive way he did his best to find out why Marlene should be going to Micklebury on a Tuesday, instead of going on a Thursday with Donald. His sharp eye noted the whisky bottle in Marlene's basket. Not only was she going shopping on a Tuesday instead of a Thursday, she was taking poor old Donald's whisky with her! Marlene was tight lipped and gave nothing away as she had little to say to Tater these days since the unfortunate episode with the vicar. Once on the bus, Tater sat next to her but Marlene avoided talking to him by turning around and talking to Janice in the seat behind. Janice was her neighbour who lived on an eighty acre farm along the lane. Marlene and Janice had become good friends for Janice too came from outside the area and had suffered from the barbs of local gossip after she married David, a local farmer. They chatted comfortably during the journey to Micklebury. While Marlene had her back to him, talking over her shoulder to Janice, Tater removed the whisky bottle from her shopping basket and secreted it in the inside pocket of his baggy sports jacket.

Once in Micklebury Marlene made her way to the surgery and after a short wait was introduced to the doctor. She explained why she had come and the doctor made some routine enquiries and finally asked if she had brought a sample of her urine with her.

Marlene reached into her basket and was astonished to find that the whisky bottle was missing. Suddenly, she burst out into peals of laughter.

'Oh! I hope he had a good swig of it.' She chortled, then seeing the doctor's mystified face she explained that she had brought a urine sample with her in a whisky bottle that someone had stolen it and she had a very good idea who it might be. The Doctor smiled.

'Well, that laugh will have done you a power of good,' he said, 'but you can give me a sample while you are here just to be on the safe side.' The doctor wrote out a prescription for Marlene and asked her to return in a week's time if the problem had not cleared up.

Marlene did a little shopping and made her way back to the bus station to catch the bus home. She didn't tell

Donald about her visit to the doctor and she thought little more about it.

A few days later Marlene took the eggs to the village shop as usual and whilst there she bought a knitting pattern for an outfit for a new born baby and took quite a lot of trouble over buying some baby wool, settling at last for a pretty shade of lemon as she didn't know what sex the baby was to be. Mary Goodings served her without making any comment and Marlene nodded to Joan Wainwright who came into the shop.

'Morning Mrs Wainwright,' she said as she left.

Next morning there was a knock on the back door just as Marlene was making herself a cup of tea. She opened the door to find Janice on the doorstep.

'Come in. You're just in time for a cuppa,' said Marlene setting out another cup and saucer. Janice sat down and nibbled a biscuit and she and Marlene chatted about the weather, the garden, how well the hens were laying, how much jam they had made, who was to give a talk at the next WI meeting until finally Marlene looked at Janice and said in her usual direct way.

'Janice you didn't come here just to gossip. You never sit and chat at this time of the day. You're too busy. What are you here for?'

Janice blushed.

'I've come to be nosy, Marlene. You see I couldn't help seeing you come out of the doctor's surgery on Tuesday. Then when I was in the shop just now Mary

Goodings was telling everyone that you are pregnant, saying that you have been in the shop buying wool for baby clothes. I thought I would let you know what is being said.'

Marlene looked thoughtful.

'They have put two and two together and made half a dozen again,' she said. 'I can promise you Janice that as far as I know I am not pregnant. I'm knitting a little outfit for a girlfriend who has just left work to have a baby, but don't say anything to anyone and I just might have a bit of fun over this. Thanks for telling me.'

Janice left and Marlene set about her daily routine, her mind busily turning over ways of convincing the village that she really was pregnant. Over the next three weeks every time Marlene went to the village she wore loose clothing and she pushed her stomach out so that she could be, might be, almost certainly was pregnant! Towards the end of the third week she even tucked some rolled up stockings into the top of her pants, patting and pushing until she had achieved just the effect she was after, and it was this final touch that convinced the village women that Marlene was pregnant. Thelma Rowbottom, the expert on such matters, pronounced that Marlene was carrying twins and that they would be twin boys for she was carrying it all out front and none on the hips.

Tater was well aware of the rumours but took little notice of them until he heard that Thelma had spoken. If Thelma said Marlene was pregnant, then it had to be true.

That night Tater accosted Donald in the pub. Donald was quietly enjoying his half of bitter and a game of darts when Tater slapped him on the shoulder congratulating him loudly.

'So you've tupped 'er at last then. You've put 'er down to calve! I reckon news like that calls for drinks all round.'

There was an expectant hush in the bar for they were all well aware of what Tater was talking about, all except Donald, and the regulars were also well aware that Donald rarely bought anyone as much as a half of bitter.

'Whatever are you on about?' Donald gasped, having choked on his beer. 'Who's calving?'

'Why Marlene, of course; 'tis all around the village. Expecting twins, I hear.' Tater looked at Donald in surprise. 'You mean to say you don't know? It's been common knowledge for the past week at least.'

Donald hurriedly finished his beer and made his way home. How could she be pregnant he thought. They'd only done it the once. Surely she couldn't be having twins! Glory be! Heavens above! How much would twins cost?

When Marlene decided to play her little trick on the village women it hadn't occurred to her that Donald would be conned into thinking her pregnant too. When

Donald arrived home she was sitting comfortable by the window catching the last of the evening light as she knitted the little baby outfit. She could see that something had disturbed him. He kept looking at her over yesterday's paper that he had picked up and was pretending to read. Finally he spoke.

'Who be you knitting for then?' he asked anxiously. 'I can't recall anyone in the family who is expecting.'

Marlene gave Donald a keen glance and noticed that he was looking quite pale.

'It's a little outfit for one of my girlfriends at work. She is leaving to have a baby and I thought I would like to send her something. Did you think I was expecting then Donald?' she asked innocently.

''Tis all around the village that you're carrying twins. Thelma Rowbottom has it that it is twin boys and they'll be late.'

'Oh good,' said Marlene, wrapping up the knitting and putting it to one side. 'I was hoping they would think that. I can stop putting a cushion under my belt now then.'

Donald looked across at Marlene. With her hair tied back instead of put up in a bun, and her face and arms tanned from working in the sun Marlene was a different woman from the one he had first met in Aylesbury. If she could fool Thelma and the village women like that there was more in her than met the eye he thought. He preferred the new Marlene to the smart, efficient London secretary he had married.

'Next time you decide to play a trick like that, just let me in on the secret first will you?' he said plaintively, then chuckled.

'You fooled 'em properly that time girl!'

Chapter Eighteen
Cousin Sossie's Visit

Early in September Marlene's cousin Sossie wrote to Marlene asking if she could come for a visit. In the few days before Sossie was due to arrive Marlene cleaned the cottage until it was spotless. She had made the most of her one hundred and forty pound treasure trove and had made the cottage look homely and attractive. With Donald's help she had taken the carpets from the living room and the dining room outside and had beaten out the dust and grit that had accumulated in them over the years. By swapping them over she now had a relatively unworn carpet in the living room and the shabby, worn one hidden by the dining room table. She had made new curtains, bought some rugs and painted, cleaned and polished everything in the house and had at last had her bits and pieces of furniture sent down from London. Her double bed and single bed had replaced Donald's ancient cast iron ones which had been dismantled and put away in the shed. Cast iron bed heads came in very handy occasionally for a temporary way of blocking a glat in the hedge. Donald had breathed a sigh of relief when the truck arrived for until then he had never really believed that Marlene intended to stay.

Donald and Marlene still had their differences of opinion, inevitably over money. There had been quite a major argument over a very minor incident. Marlene had objected to using torn up newspaper for toilet paper and had bought a toilet roll holder, nailed it to the wall of the toilet and hung a roll of soft pink toilet paper upon it. Donald regarded this as quite unwarranted extravagance and said so. Marlene's reply had been to the effect that she had not realised just how dreadfully poor they were and promised to economise much more carefully in the kitchen. This she did by serving up meals of watery mince, overdone cabbage and mashed potatoes with no delicious dessert to follow. When Donald queried this she pointed out that puddings cost money and used up valuable eggs that she could sell. It was a ploy that she used every time that Donald complained of extravagance and he soon learned that it was better to say nothing and to agonise in silence and eat well, rather than to complain and suffer the consequences.

On the day of Sossie's arrival Marlene was just getting ready to walk into the village to meet the coach when a car pulled up in the driveway. Sossie had taken driving lessons and bought herself a Morris Minor. Marlene was most impressed, as Sossie had intended her to be, and they spent the few days of her visit driving around the countryside. The weather was glorious with a nip in the air in the mornings followed by warm sunny days. The countryside was looking at its best, the picturesque black and white cottages surrounded by gardens filled with dahlias and chrysanthemums, the orchards laden with fruit and the red and white Hereford cattle fat and sleek in the fields. Sossie was enchanted and could at last understand why Marlene had taken the plunge and made the break from her life in London.

One day they drove through the lanes to Ludlow where they explored the ruins of the castle and wandered through the market where Sossie bought a piece of home cooked ham and some farmhouse butter as her contribution to the housekeeping. She was only too well aware that Donald considered having a visitor staying in the house to be a wasteful extravagance and the two women were careful to be home in time to have his meal ready as they did not want to upset him and have future visits forbidden.

On another day they drove to Hereford to look around the magnificent old cathedral and see the chained library. For Marlene it was a welcome break from her months of backbreaking work and was the nearest she was likely to get to having a holiday. If Sossie's driving was a little erratic Marlene was not the one to notice and Sossie suggested she should ask Donald if she could take some lessons and learn to drive his old pick-up. Marlene thought it might be a good idea but decided to wait for the right moment before asking him.

On the last evening of Sossie's visit Donald, Marlene and Sossie strolled up the lane to the village pub, where they enjoyed a game of darts. Sossie drank two half pints of the strong local cider, known as wicky, and was mildly tiddly when they walked back down the lane. She skipped about and sang and behaved very girlishly. Donald rather liked her, he considered her to be a cuddly little armful and had enjoyed having her to stay in the house. It had been an interesting experience, living in a house with two women after so many years of bachelorhood.

When they reached the cottage Marlene set about making some supper, she laid the table and put out the carving knife and fork for Donald to carve the piece of ham that Sossie had bought. She set out homemade bread, the farmhouse butter and homemade tomato chutney. It was a simple delicious meal. Donald was sitting by the table tamping tobacco into his pipe when Marlene went into the pantry to fetch the cheese. All of a sudden Sossie leapt to her feet, grabbed the carving knife and fork and stood over Donald brandishing them wildly.

'Drop your trousers!' she commanded loudly. 'Your bellybutton hasn't been cleaned out since you were a babe in arms. Let me clean it now!' she ordered flashing the carving knife and fork dangerously close to his head.

Poor Donald was dumfounded. He thought she had suddenly gone completely mad. He leapt to his feet, his pipe clenched in his teeth, his hands gripping his trousers firmly and made a dive out of the kitchen door. Sossie followed him still clutching the carving knife and fork, and whooping like a madwoman. Donald took off through the home paddock and out into the field, going for his life with Sossie shrieking along behind, her plump little legs covering the ground with amazing speed. Marlene leant against the door post and watched as the cattle in the field got up from their night time resting places, the hens set up a cackle of alarm in the hen house and a cock pheasant, disturbed from his roost in the spinney disappeared noisily into the night. Donald finally made enough ground to get back to the house and he dived into the outside toilet, slamming and bolting the door behind him. Sossie returned to the kitchen and slumped, panting and laughing into a chair.

'Oh! That was fun,' she gasped between breaths.

'He'll never forgive you,' said Marlene and Donald never did. He remained firmly convinced that Sossie was quietly but completely mad and he stayed well away from her and had little to do with her after this night.

Chapter Nineteen
Apple Picking

It was after Sossie's visit that Donald and Marlene had their first really major row. Sossie had not missed an opportunity to comment on the primitive sanitary arrangements and washing facilities in the cottage, which Marlene had done her best to gloss over. However, when Janice invited Marlene down to her house to view Janice's newly installed bathroom, complete with flush toilet and heated towel rail, Marlene's dissatisfaction came to a head once again. She had done her very best with the cottage but there was no way that she herself could raise enough money to put in a proper bathroom.

The final straw had come one Friday night when she had settled herself into the little zinc tub by the stove, hair put up out of the way, enjoying the warmth of the water on muscles stiff from a long day in the garden. Just this once Marlene had overlooked to lock the back door and Tater, who had visited the house regularly on a

Friday evening like an old fox checking a henrun hoping to catch a glimpse of Marlene in the bath, found the door unlocked and walked boldly in.

Marlene's shriek had brought Donald running from the living room and suddenly Marlene's bathroom had been invaded by not one, but two, men. Both men caught more than a glimpse of her pink nakedness as she stood up and grabbed a towel and for a moment or two there was pandemonium as Marlene shouted at both of them to get out, Donald shouted at Tater and Tater shouted his apologies as he beat a hasty retreat.

Marlene decided to tackle Donald about it again after they had their evening meal and were sitting in front of one of the first fires of the winter, but Donald was adamant that he did not have the money to spend on the cottage, and even if he had he wouldn't spend it as he was quite happy with the way things were. He felt a little more confident now that Marlene's furniture had arrived and she had settled in. Marlene went off to bed in a temper and Donald went out to work in the shed, tinkering with the car until he saw that she had put the light out. He crept into bed beside her and they lay stiffly each on their own side of the bed, careful not to touch each other.

Donald had been out picking damsons during the day and as he was very partial to damsons he had eaten plenty while he was picking them, and he awoke with a griping pain in his stomach. Marlene was dimly aware of him leaving the room as he got out of bed to go to the toilet. Suddenly she sat bolt upright as she heard a muffled explosion downstairs. Whatever was that? She crept out of bed and down the stairs and was horrified to see a dark red stain seeping out from under the cupboard door. Donald must have taken the twelve bore into the cupboard and shot himself! She was standing transfixed with horror looking at the slowly widening stain when the back door rattled and Donald came back into the kitchen, hitching up his pyjama trousers and hurrying to get back into his warm bed. He was quite bemused when Marlene hurled herself across the kitchen and threw her arms around his neck.

'Whatever's come over you?' Donald asked, patting her gently on the shoulder. 'What's wrong?'

'I thought you had shot yourself,' sobbed Marlene, pointing to the red stain which was spreading across the kitchen. 'I heard this explosion and thought that was blood and I thought you had taken your gun into the cupboard and shot yourself.'

When Donald opened the cupboard they saw the reason for the explosion. Two bottles of elderberry wine had fermented and exploded, leaving a mess of glass and wine to be cleared up in the morning.

Marlene was up and about early next day as she had to clear up the mess in the kitchen before she left to go to work in the apple orchards. She was working in the local orchards picking and packing apples and enjoyed the work and the extra money it brought in. During the summer she had tried strawberry picking, which was back breaking work, and currant picking but, of the three, it was the apple picking which she enjoyed. Marlene was gradually being accepted by the village women and had made several friends amongst them. She went to the Women's Institute meeting each month and sold some of her produce through the Wl shop in Micklebury. Today Marlene was working in the sheds, packing the apples into boxes ready for the market, and she worked deftly with her big capable hands. As she worked she listened to the sound of the wind rising outside and thought about their own apples waiting to be picked in the little orchard. The apple trees were big and old and you needed a ladder to reach the fruit at the top of the trees. Marlene decided to ask Donald if he would help her to pick the fruit tomorrow as the forecast on the radio was for gales for the next few days and the apples would be spoilt if they all came down as windfalls.

That evening when Marlene asked Donald to help her pick their apples he replied that he was too busy to help, but he would ask Tater if he could lend a hand. Marlene decided to go ahead and pick all the fruit she could reach anyway and she was busy working in the orchard when Tater arrived with the long ladder. He set it up in the highest tree but when Marlene suggested he should be the one to go up the ladder he flatly refused.

'I've got no 'ead for 'eights,' he said emphatically. 'There's no way I be goin' up there.'

Marlene emptied the pocket of her big apple-picking apron and climbed the ladder herself, stepping off it into the top of the tree, which was already beginning to sway as the wind picked up in force. She held on with one hand and picked the big Bramley cookers with the other. The apples were lovely sound fruit and would keep them in apple pies and tarts for many months in the winter. With her apron full of apples Marlene went to step back on to the ladder, only to find that Tater had removed it from the tree and laid it on the ground.

'That'll teach you to put wee in a whisky bottle!' he yelled at her venomously before he lifted his leg over his bicycle and pedalled off in the direction of the village. Marlene shouted and pleaded with him to return and help her down from the tree but he simply gave a last wave of his hand as he pedalled out of sight. Marlene was left to roost in the top of the apple tree, which was beginning to sway like a ship on a rough sea, for half an hour before Donald came pedalling along the lane on his way home for his mid-day meal and rescued her from her predicament.

'Why should Tater go and do a thing like that?' wondered Donald as he enjoyed his cup of tea. 'I know you and he don't get along too well but something must have really upset him for him to leave you like that!'

Marlene sighed. 'I can explain it,' she said and told Donald of her visit to the doctor and her need to take a urine sample with her.

'Tater must have thought I'd got some of your whisky in my shopping bag and he stole it from me when I was on the bus. It looks as if he must have drunk it,' she said, keeping her face perfectly straight. 'At least he shouted something about a whisky bottle when he left me in the tree.' She paused thoughtfully. 'I didn't actually mind it sitting up there. It was like being on a sailing ship.' She grinned wickedly. 'I bet he hasn't drunk much whisky lately. It couldn't have happened to a nicer fellow.'

She hummed happily to herself as she cleared the table and started to wash the dishes, leaving Donald yet again to wonder about the woman he had married.

Chapter Twenty
A Visit from The Diddicoys

One morning Marlene was in the kitchen doing some baking when Tater arrived to collect some potatoes that Donald had put aside for him. He stood looking enviously into the freshly painted kitchen that smelled deliciously of newly baked bread.

'Mornin Marlene,' he said. 'Donald said to tell you that the diddicoys be comin' around and to sort out any old rubbish you don't want.'

'What's a diddicoy when he's around?' asked Marlene, not really wanting to waste any breath talking to Tater.

'I suppose you'd call 'em tinkers in your part of the world,' said Tater. 'They comes around every now and then selling pegs and taking any rags and rubbish you don't want.'

He waited until Marlene turned her back and went into the pantry and then sneaked into the kitchen and slipped four fresh rock cakes into his pocket.

Tater was well aware that Donald wouldn't give the diddicoys the peelings of his nails, let alone any of his precious hoard of useful tack. He was hoping that Marlene would give away something that Donald valued and land herself in hot water. Although he never guessed it he succeeded beyond his wildest dreams.

'Thanks for telling me,' said Marlene curtly. 'I expect it's time you were on your way. I've no time to stand here gossiping to the likes of you.'

Tater loaded the sack of potatoes on his bike and disappeared up the lane, munching contentedly on a rock cake as he went.

When Marlene had finished her baking she set about sorting out some of the old things that she was keen to get rid of. She put the old curtains that she had taken down in a pile, added some of the fairground trophies her late mother-in-law had won, and went upstairs to check through their wardrobe. Her own clothes were in good condition as she had had a good turn out before she had married, but there were some of Donald's that were worn to threads. She put aside a couple of ancient hand-knitted jumpers that were past saving and then took a good look at his suit. She hadn't really done anything to it since the day of Vi's wedding and when she laid it out and checked it over it became plain that it was past repairing. The left knee and elbow were torn and the right hand jacket pocket had ripped away where it had caught in the handlebars of the bicycle. Donald would moan dreadfully about buying a new suit but if this one was gone he wouldn't be able to wear it again.

Marlene was about to roll the suit up with the jumpers when she noticed a bulge in the left hand side of the jacket. She checked the inside pocket again and then realised there was a hole in the lining which, on investigation, proved to hold a roll of banknotes. She pulled it out and sat and counted it, one thousand six hundred and forty-seven pounds ten shillings in a motley collection of notes, rolled up tight in a rubber band – Donald's life savings.

Marlene took the money and weighed it thoughtfully in her hand. She ran down to the kitchen and put it in an old stone pickle jar in the very back of the pantry while she considered what to do with it. She rolled up the suit and the other clothes she was discarding and took them down to the kitchen just as a brightly decorated Bedford truck pulled up, announcing the arrival of the diddicoys. Marlene bought two dozen pegs and handed over her pile of discarded goods to the swarthy men who stood on her doorstep. Then she made herself a cup of tea and sat down in the kitchen thinking hard about the money she had found.

Donald had steadfastly maintained during the whole of their marriage that he had absolutely no money and after a while Marlene had come to believe him. Marlene, in reply had told him that she too was penniless, which was not entirely true. For a while she considered telling

Donald that she had not found the money in the suit, then she could do what she had done with the money from behind the picture frames and have a bathroom and toilet put in but this time her conscience would not allow her to do it, so she decided to leave the money where it was and wait and see what happened when Donald realised it was missing.

It was four days before Donald went to add some cash to his little hoard. Marlene saw him go upstairs and heard him open the wardrobe door. She waited for the explosion which she knew would come. Donald came thundering down the stairs and burst into the kitchen.

'Where's my suit? Where's my suit? It isn't in the cupboard,' he shouted. 'What have you done with it?'

'I gave it to the tinkers,' said Marlene and before she could add any words of explanation Donald shot out of the back door and leapt into his old car and roared out of the yard. He didn't come home until about 11.30 that night, well after Marlene had gone to bed and the next morning he sat, grey and depressed, at the breakfast table picking at his food.

'What's the matter, Donald?' Marlene asked.

'I've lost all my money, t'was in the lining of my suit. You had no right to go giving my stuff away like that.' He glared at Marlene angrily.

'How much have you lost, then?' asked Marlene innocently.

'About two hundred pound,' Donald lied. 'I chased after the diddicoys all the way the other side of Hereford but they said they found no money in it. Course they would say that, wouldn't they?' He held his head in his hands almost in tears.

Marlene went into the pantry and retrieved the roll of notes from the pickle jar.

'Is this what you are looking for?' she asked, keeping a firm hold on the money.

'That's it!' Donald leapt to his feet and reached over to grab the cash.

'Why didn't you tell me you'd got it? Why let me go tearing all over the countryside looking for it when it was here all the time?'

'You didn't give me a chance to,' said Marlene. 'Now just sit down and let's have a little chat about this, shall we? There is sixteen hundred and forty seven pounds ten shillings here, not two hundred like you said. You've told me ever since we got married how broke you are, and I don't think you've been telling me the truth! I've got a proposition to put to you and I think you had better sit there and listen to me.'

Donald sat down meekly, wondering what was coming – something about that dratted bathroom he had no doubt, He watched anxiously as Marlene stuffed the roll of notes into her brassiere well out of his reach.

'I've got to be truthful with you Donald,' Marlene began. 'I like living here and being married to you. There is only one fly in the ointment and you know what that is.'

'I know,' said Donald heavily, 'no bathroom, no flush toilet, no hot water.'

'Yes,' said Marlene, 'and as far as you were concerned, no money to put them in. Now you haven't been truthful with me and I haven't been quite fair with you. I do have some money put by so if you will give me five hundred pounds of this money towards a bathroom and flush toilet, then I will pay the rest. It's a fair offer for you got me her under false pretences in the first place, you know.'

Donald sighed deeply and sat thinking hard. 'Look, m'dear, just give me my money back now and then when you have got some prices for putting in the bathroom we'll talk about it again,' he said hopefully.

Marlene stood up and walked across to the woodstove. She lifted the lid and poked at the fire, put her hand into her blouse and withdrew the cash.

'Five hundred pounds now, Donald, or the lot goes in here,' she said emphatically.

'You win,' said Donald bitterly, as he watched Marlene peel off and count out five hundred pounds.

'How do I know you won't take off for London with it and leave me in the lurch?'

'I won't, I promise you,' said Marlene, rolling up the rest of the notes and handing them to Donald. 'Cheer up,' she said smiling at him. 'Who knows once we've got a bathroom in we might even start living like a real married couple with a bit of nooky now and then!'

Donald choked as he drew on his pipe, and looked at her through his watering eyes. It had been a mistake marrying this London woman. No good Herefordshire girl would treat her husband like this.

Chapter Twenty-One
Evans the Mouse

Marlene wasted no time contacting builders and tradesmen about putting in her bathroom. She planned to turn the little upstairs box room into the bathroom and to have the outside toilet converted to a flush toilet. She filled out forms for the Council and finally arranged for the plumber who had installed Janice's bathroom to do hers immediately after Christmas.

Marlene worked with a light heart, helping Donald in the garden where they lifted the root vegetables, the carrots, parsnips, turnips and swedes and buried them in a clamp to protect them from the winter frosts. Donald had his cabbages and Brussels sprouts in the garden and plenty of dry firewood stacked in the shed as they prepared themselves for the cold winter months ahead.

The weather had changed from the lovely Indian summer weather of Sossie's visit and they had had a long period of gales and heavy rain which made them appreciate the snug warmth of their little cottage.

The mice appreciated the snug warmth too and moved into the house with the onset of the wet weather. Marlene hated them and set traps regularly to catch as many as she could.

One morning, as dawn was breaking, Marlene stirred in her sleep and slowly drifted into consciousness. Her eyes still closed she heard the rooster challenging the world from his perch in the henhouse and the first stirrings of the birds in the holly bush outside the window. Sleepily Marlene counted through the days of the week and happily established that it was Sunday morning. She opened her eyes and looked at the clock. Ten to seven, time for another ten minutes in bed before she made a cup of tea. She closed her eyes and snuggled down into the bedclothes, then her eyes flew open again. A mouse sat grooming its whiskers delicately beside the alarm clock on her bedside table.

'There's a mouse!' Marlene's panic stricken voice rent the morning air and her sharp elbow thudded painfully into Donald's back between his shoulder blades.

'THERE'S A MOUSE!' Marlene's voice rose an octave as she placed her bony feet in the small of Donald's back and shot him out of bed. He hovered horizontally for a moment before landing with a thud on the rag rug that covered the lino. He picked himself up and turned to curse Marlene, but took one look at her terrified face and realised he would be wasting his breath. Marlene was by now standing on the bed, one hand clutching her flannelette nightie closely around her legs, the other held in the air directing Donald as to the whereabouts of the mouse. Donald reached into the wardrobe for a walking stick and began to lay about him.

'It's under the dressing table' – *thwack* – 'it's by the washstand' – *thud* – 'it's running up the curtain.' *Swipe!*

As Marlene's voice rose so did Donald's temper until he was laying about him with the walking stick in a series of frenzied lashes, culminating in one almighty swipe as the mouse ran under the marble topped washstand. Donald missed his footing as the rag rug shot from under his feet and he landed heavily on the lino – covered floor, hitting his face on the washstand as he fell. The beleaguered mouse seized its chance and shot through a tiny crack in the skirting board and Marlene, seeing it escape stepped down from the bed to help Donald to his feet.

He was a sorry sight with his right eye closing rapidly and blood spurting vigorously from his badly battered nose. Marlene handed him the towel from the washstand and helped him to sit on the side of the bed. Donald rolled his one good eye beseechingly in her direction.

'Go and get a cold key,' he muttered through the thick folds of the towel. 'Get a cold key and put it down me back.'

Marlene looked at him blankly for a moment but the expression of mounting fury in the solitary good eye galvanised her into activity. She picked up her nightie above her knees and sprinted out of the bedroom, covered the landing in a couple of strides and pounded down the stairs, skidding on the mat at the bottom and flailing her arm to corner hard into the kitchen. She crossed the kitchen at full speed, delved into her refrigerator and seized a bag of her frozen peas. Turning she repeated her record breaking performance up the stairs, moving faster than she had done since she was in the Under 14 hockey team at school. Arriving back in the bedroom, gasping for breath, she tore the bag of frozen peas open with her teeth. Donald sat on the bed, his eyes closed, the towel clutched to his nose.

'Put it down me back,' he said as he leaned forward. Marlene seized the collar of his pyjamas, pulled it back and shot the entire bag of frozen peas down Donald's back in one go. Donald stiffened and arched his back, his eye flew open.

'What was that?' he gasped.

'Frozen peas,' said Marlene, looking bewildered. 'That's what you said. Fetch some cold peas and put them down your back.'

Donald winced. 'Don't you know anything you silly old cow? I said a COLD KEY. That's what you always put down someone's back when they have a nosebleed, a COLD KEY!'

He stood up gingerly and a fusillade of frozen peas rattled to the floor.

Silly old cow indeed! After all that effort too. Marlene pulled herself up to her full height, tied her dressing gown belt tightly around her and thrust her feet into her slippers.

'I'll go and put the kettle on,' she said huffily and stalked out of the room.

Donald peered into the mirror and looked bleakly at his injured face. He shouldn't have called her that. He would be on gristly mince and lumpy semolina for weeks now until she got over it.

Tenderly he sponged his face in the basin and looked again at his swollen nose and classic black eye. All over a mouse too! They'd have some fun over this at the pub. He wouldn't be 'Evans the Stone House' in the village any more, he'd be 'Evans the Mouse' for sure.

Chapter Twenty-Two
Christmas in Millbrook

Christmas was approaching and Marlene was anxious to get her shopping and baking done in good time, for she had been tending a large pen of cockerels, fattening them especially for Christmas and there would be a hectic rush at the last minute to have the poultry dressed and ready. She baked her Christmas cake and boiled the pudding at the beginning of the month and made up some jars of mincemeat that she put away in the pantry to mature. She smiled to herself when she recalled her first efforts at Christmas baking when she was only twelve and her mother had been in hospital. Determined to make a pudding and a cake the young Marlene had set about it without either recipe or scales. She had made up an enormous bowlful of a mixture containing everything she could think of (including about half a bottle of her father's best old brandy). She had divided the mixture into two, boiled half of it for a pudding and baked the rest for a cake. The results had been edible but quite unlike any pudding or cake she had ever tasted. Thank goodness her cooking had improved since then.

For Donald's Christmas present Marlene had knitted him a new jumper in a heather-mixture wool with a cable pattern up the front, and for Tater Marlene had found a set of the three brass monkeys, Hear no Evil, Speak no Evil and See no Evil, that was sitting on the white elephant stall at the local school fete. The significance of the gift was entirely lost upon Tater, however, for when he received it he examined it carefully and promised to pass it on to Mary the Shop as she was such a terrible gossip!

Tater's gift to Donald and Marlene was a very large garden gnome, gaudily painted in the brightest colours that Tater had been able to find. He knew perfectly well Marlene would hate it as he had caught her putting an ancient gnome that had belonged to Donald's mother into the dustbin when Donald was out.

Donald realised rather belatedly that he would be expected to give Marlene a gift for Christmas. He had totally overlooked her birthday, so she had ignored his, which occurred three weeks after hers. It had been an unfortunate oversight that he had not been allowed to forget so he was anxious to do the right thing at Christmas and keep out of trouble. After much pondering Donald recalled the little gold brooch amongst his mother's trinkets and decided to give it to Marlene for a Christmas gift.

A few days before Christmas Donald brought home a little Christmas tree, cut some holly from the bush by the house and together they decorated the cottage, giving it a festive air.

On Christmas Eve, when the last of the poultry had been collected by her customers, Marlene walked to the church to join in the carol singing. This year, for the first time for many years, the vicar had revived the old custom of village carol services, hoping to raise some money towards the Church Organ Fund. He had organised his choir members and they had been practising after evensong for the past month. There was a keen local group of handbell players who were going to join in and posters had been put up around the village giving details of the recitals. They were planning to sing in the old market square first, then walk up the hill and sing outside the Red Lion and finally walk about a mile out of the village to the Manor where Colonel Lloyd-Bobbington was having a Christmas house-party. Colonel Lloyd-Bobbington was the church's most generous benefactor.

The weather was cold and dry with a hint of frost in the air and the carol singers were well wrapped in their winter clothes. The concert in the market place was well received with people coming out of their homes to listen to their favourite carols and to join in. The vicar weighed the collection boxes hopefully after they had been passed around.

The group walked briskly up to the Red Lion carrying their old fashioned lanterns, the vicar skirting around the rear of his procession rounding up the stragglers and the younger choir boys who were more interested in playing with their torches than getting to the Red Lion. He had promised their parents he would return them safely and he didn't want to lose any of them on the way.

The carols outside the Red Lion were again well received with quite a crowd of people coming to listen and join in. Once it was over the group set out to walk the mile to the Manor, the vicar once again having to round up one or two stragglers, this time male members of the choir who had slipped into the pub for a 'quick one'. They walked quickly, stamping their feet to get warm and chattering and laughing between themselves.

When they reached the Manor they grouped themselves around the French windows leading to the drawing room so that Colonel Lloyd-Bobbington and his guests could gather around and listen to the carols without exposing themselves to the cold night air. The Colonel turned off the lights in the drawing room so that it was lit only by the lights on the Christmas tree and by the glow from a blazing log fire. With the choir grouped outside under the starry sky, their faces lit by torch and lantern light it was like a scene from a Victorian Christmas card.

The choir launched into 'Hark the Herald Angels Sing' with enthusiasm, knowing that hot mince pies and rum punch or lemonade would be waiting for them after they had finished their recital.

By this time the younger members of the choir, bored by the third recital and over-excited at the prospect of opening their presents on Christmas Day, began to get fidgety. Young Brian Griffiths dared Billy West to turn on the tap of the rainwater butt just as Ned Jones, the village baritone, was singing his solo opening to 'Once in Royal David's City'.

'Who's a'piddling?' Ned demanded, his fruity voice carrying all too clearly in the cold night air, and a ripple of laughter came from the party guests in the house much to the vicar's annoyance. The vicar moved around to stand between Brian and Billy.

'No one's piddling Ned, now let's take that again from the beginning shall we?' he said, glaring at the young lads and whispering a somewhat un-Christian threat in their ears, for the vicar was hoping that the Colonel and his guests would make a substantial donation to the church funds.

When the recital was finally over and the mince pies and rum punch and lemonade had been enjoyed the choir made their way back to Millbrook tired and happy and looking forward to their Christmas celebrations.

Christmas at the Stone House was a quiet and relaxed affair filled with good food, and was a time for reflection over the past year and of plans for the year to come.

Chapter Twenty-Three
Old Bill's Birthday

Immediately after the New Year celebrations Marlene laid plans with the plumber for the best and quickest way for the bathroom to be installed, for Marlene was anxious that it should cause as little disruption as possible as Donald was still as frostily opposed to the idea as ever.

The actual installation of the bath and wash-basin in the box room was a minor consideration. The chief problem was how to remove the cold-water tank from over the stairs and install it in the attic. It was finally decided that some of the roofing slates would have to be removed and some of the timber cut to allow the tank, along with the hot water service, to be fitted in the attic. Marlene knew that Donald would never allow a single slate to be taken from the roof so it was decided that this part of the job should be done after Donald had left to go to market on Thursday. Marlene prayed fervently for a fine day and for the job to go ahead without any hitches, and her prayers were answered.

When Donald returned home late in the afternoon the tank and water heater were installed safely in the attic with hot and cold running water to the kitchen sink. The transformation of the outside toilet from an old bucket under a wooden seat to a modern porcelain flush toilet was planned with similar military precision and the final touches were completed without Donald being inconvenienced in any way. The only grouse he had was that the plumbers had dug up a part of his lawn to install the septic tank but Marlene carefully replaced all the turf and tended it lovingly so that the scars soon began to heal.

Marlene was ecstatic at having a proper bathroom and toilet at last, but for a while Donald persisted in boiling the kettle on the wood stove and shaving at the kitchen sink, peering into his cracked mirror and rasping away with a worn out razor blade. Marlene frustrated Donald's efforts to keep bathing in the kitchen by filling the zinc tub with wood for the fires and finally, in exasperation she threw out the cracked mirror and firmly placed his razor in the bathroom. Donald continued to mourn the loss of the soapy water for his plants and the loss of the contents of the toilet which, according to him, produced the best possible rhubarb, but he had to admit that Marlene was happier than he had ever seen her and that his house was far more comfortable and his life much improved since his marriage. Marlene for her part put aside any thoughts of returning to London and settled down to make the most of her life in the country.

One cold evening in the middle of January Marlene, instead of settling by the fire with her knitting, put on her outdoor clothes ready to go to the monthly meeting of the Woman's Institute. She poked her head around the door to see if there was any chance of Donald giving her a lift to the village but on seeing him comfortably settled by the fire with his pipe and yesterday's paper she didn't bother to ask. As she hurried up the lane Marlene wished that she had learned to drive but then again she would rather be out in the fresh air, listening to the wind in the trees and seeing the clouds scudding across the moon, than sitting in a smelly old car.

The village hall was abuzz with chatter when Marlene arrived but the meeting was soon called to order. After the business had been dealt with Mary Price showed some of her slides of her holiday in Majorca, which made the women forget for a short time the cold dark wintry conditions in the village and allowed them to bask dreamily in the sunny Mediterranean climate. Afterwards they settled down to a cup of tea and a chat and while they were talking Janice mentioned that it was Old Bill's birthday on Friday.

'I popped in to the Smithy to pick up some scissors he had been sharpening for me,' she said, 'and he had just been clearing some old papers out of his desk and found his birth certificate. He said he thought he had lost it years ago. Anyway he's going to be eighty-five on Friday.'

Old Bill was a popular member of the village. He had been a pensioner for many years and he helped out around the village doing odd jobs, seldom taking more than the price of a pint in return. The children of the village took their broken toys to him and he spent many hours repairing bicycles, tricycles and doll's prams.

'Let's give him a surprise,' said Janice. 'Let's make him a birthday cake and a jelly and take it around and surprise him.'

'He always comes to me on Fridays,' Vi Williams said in her soft lilting Welsh voice. 'He comes just after one and does a few odd jobs for me and leaves just before three. Then he goes to see old Sarah Smith to take her a bit of morning wood and see if she needs anything. He'll be home by three thirty though 'cos he can't see too well once it starts to get dark.'

Janice looked across at Vi.

'I can see the back of your house from my place, so if you hang a towel out of your bedroom window when he leaves you, I'll leave then and give Marlene a knock when I pass, and I can give Thelma a shout too.'

'And then you can put your head around the door of the shop and let me know,' said Mary Goodings.

'Do you think I could bring the children?' June Billings the schoolmistress asked. 'They are very fond of Old Bill you know and they could make him some birthday cards.'

'I can pop over when I see the children leaving the school,' said Mary Price and so it was arranged and the women settled down to discuss what food they would bring.

On Friday, as soon as Old Bill left Vi William's house, she hurried upstairs to hang out her new red bath towel, then packed a jelly in her special jelly mould in the basket of her sit-up-and-beg bicycle, put on her mac and her hat and pedalled hastily down the road.

Janice saw the bath towel flapping, took off her apron and picked up her basket which was already packed with scones and strawberry jam. She shouted and waved to Thelma, two fields away, and then hurried up the road to knock on Marlene's door. Marlene was waiting with a biscuit tin full of sausage rolls and together they hurried along the lane towards the Smithy where Old Bill lived.

Thelma picked up her basket, which held a fruit cake iced with '85 Today' on it and some candles, pulled her door to and hurried down the lane to the village, pausing to put her head around the door at the school before popping into the shop. Mary Goodings picked up a block of ice cream and some chocolate biscuits, hung a notice on the shop door 'Back in Ten Minutes' and joined in the rush to get to Old Bill's house and have his birthday tea on the table before he arrived.

Thelma spread an embroidered cloth on the table, Vi shook up the fire and put the kettle on and the women spread out their food – sausage rolls, scones and jam, jelly and ice cream, chocolate biscuits and birthday cake, it was quite a spread.

Thelma lit the candles on the cake and the children placed their cards around it. They all stood quietly waiting, the children muffling their snorts and giggles as children do when they are trying to be quiet.

Old Bill put his bike in the shed and Shep his faithful border collie, who went everywhere with him, growled as they approached the back door.

'What's the matter with you, you old fool?' asked Bill, anyone would think there was someone about.'

He pushed open the back door and blinked as his old eyes took in the scene.

'We've come to wish you a happy birthday, Bill,' said Vi.

Bill shuffled in the door and made his way to his old armchair that stood beside the stove. He sat down and looked around him, overcome with emotion. Janice handed him a cup of tea and the children sang a special song they had been rehearsing for him. Then they all sang 'Happy Birthday' and settled down to enjoy the birthday tea.

'You'll excuse me if I slip away,' Mary Goodings said afterwards, 'people do get a bit cross if I'm away more than half an hour.'

Nobody said anything but they had all waited on more than one occasion for Mary to get back from one of her 'ten minutes'. They set about the washing up and put away the rest of the food. Old Bill sat in his chair by the fire, his eyes watering a little. Shep lay at his feet with his tail thumping softly.

'Well how was that then, Bill?' asked Thelma. 'A bit better than that old kipper I see in the pantry there?'

'Ladies, it was lovely,' said Bill, 'I can't say how I feel but thank you all very much. It was a grand surprise.'

Chapter Twenty-Four
Disaster

For just a few weeks in January life in the Stone House was harmonious. Marlene was well satisfied with her new bathroom and toilet and Donald accepted the changes with as good grace as he could muster although he keenly regretted the five hundred pounds that it had cost him to buy peace in his own home.

Disaster struck in February when the weather, after a cold, wet and windy January, suddenly turned bitterly cold with hard frosts and thick snow. Donald and Marlene awoke one morning to find all the pipes frozen up, which gave Donald a heaven sent opportunity to moan about the stupidity of spending a fortune to have a bathroom and toilet fitted when they ceased to work at the first sign of a frost.

They had to resort to using the old pump in the yard to bring up water from the well and to thawing out the toilet with water heated on the woodstove before it would flush. The severe weather stayed with them for the whole of the month, freezing the ground, causing accidents on the icy roads and bringing rare wild birds flocking to Marlene's bird table to feed on the scraps that she put out for them. The trees and hedges were rimed with hoar frost and there was frost on the inside of the bedroom window each morning when they awoke. Donald kept the woodstove in the kitchen well supplied with wood and they stayed warm and comfortable in the cottage in spite of the bitter cold.

At the very end of February the freeze showed signs of breaking and Donald and Marlene went into Micklebury to shop. The market had been cancelled but they were running low on supplies and Marlene had eggs and some home baked goods to sell in the Wl shop so they decided to make the journey.

It wasn't until after one in the afternoon that they returned to the cottage. This was the first day that the sun had warmed up enough for the ice and snow to begin to thaw and the trees began to drip. Indeed it was almost warm in the sun which made a welcome change.

When they got back to the cottage Marlene went upstairs to take off her outdoor clothes and tidy her hair before she set about getting a meal on the table. As she went into their bedroom she was taken aback to see the light flickering on and off. Marlene watched it with a puzzled frown until she realised that a steady trickle of water was running down the flex of the light and dripping into the centre of their double bed.

'Oh Lord!' She dropped her coat and ran back downstairs to the kitchen.

'Donald, Donald,' she cried urgently, 'there's water in the bedroom. I think you had better go up into the attic and have a look and see what's happening!'

Donald dashed out to the shed to get the stepladder and they hurried upstairs to the landing. Donald climbed the steps, lifted the trapdoor to the attic and peered in.

'Get me a torch quickly,' he snapped as he peered into the darkness.

Marlene rushed to the bedroom and snatched the torch from beside the bed. As Donald shone the torch he could see that the copper pipes under the cold water tank, frozen during the cold weather, had come apart at the joint and water was running out steadily. He scrambled up into the attic and stuck his thumb hastily into the pipe to stop the flow of water. His knowledge of plumbing was limited. He snatched at the first idea that came into his head.

'Marlene,' he shouted, 'outside the greenhouse there is a hose. Cut a piece off and bring it up here and I'll feed the water back into the tank.'

'Right,' said Marlene scrambling down the stepladder. She ran down the stairs to the kitchen, grabbed a carving knife and hurried up the garden to where the hose lay. She hacked off a length of hose and holding one end in each hand she ran back into the house, up the stairs and panted up the stepladder to the attic.

'Here you are,' she gasped, handing the hose to Donald who removed his thumb from the pipe and pushed one end of the hose over it. He held the hose up, intending to feed the other end into the tank. It wasn't until he held it up above his head that the water pushed all the ice which was in the hose out and it cascaded all over him. The icy water knocked the breath out of him for a moment, but when it came back his language was not fit to be heard. To make matters worse Marlene had not cut a long enough piece of hose for Donald to be able to feed the water into the tank so he stood there soaking wet, with a fountain of icy water gushing out of the end of the green hose, swearing furiously.

By this time Marlene was seriously alarmed.

'When they put the plumbing in they put a tap behind the door in the pantry. I'll run and turn it off,' she said as Donald once again stuffed his thumb into the copper pipe.

Marlene tumbled down the stepladder and hurtled down the stairs to the kitchen. Once in the pantry she turned the tap as hard as she could, then ran breathlessly up the stairs. She stood at the bottom of the stepladder.

'Is that better?' she called. 'Has it stopped?'

'You fool,' wailed Donald, 'you've turned the bloody thing full on! Go and turn it the other way!'

Poor Marlene fled down the stairs yet again and turned the tap as fast as she could in the other direction. It was more than she dared do to stick her head in the attic again for by this time Donald was soaking wet, freezing cold and in a towering temper. All he could say when he finally did come into the kitchen was 'I told you, you stupid woman, that there is no reason at all to have WATER in the house!'

'I'll phone the plumber,' said Marlene unhappily and disappeared hastily out of the door.

'And you'll pay for him!' Donald roared after her as she hurried up the road.

Chapter Twenty-Five
Marlene Learns to Milk

It was weeks before Donald simmered down and stopped carping about the stupidity of having a bathroom installed in the house. The ultimate insult of having his ceilings damaged, his bed soaked and his favourite armchair drenched, for the water had run through the bed and down through the ceiling into his chair, after he had laid out five hundred pounds to have the bathroom fitted when he didn't want it in the first place, had upset him badly and he didn't miss a single opportunity to say so.

Their wedding anniversary came and went, forgotten by Donald and not mentioned by Marlene and only marked by a card from Uncle Tom and Aunty Glad. However, once the spring weather set in and the planting in the garden was in full swing life gradually got back to normal.

One day when Donald pedalled back into the yard after spending the morning helping Alf Jenkins at Burbank Farm Marlene saw an oilskin bag tied to the front of his bicycle. There was nothing unusual about this except that the bag was wriggling and squirming!

'Whatever have you got in their Donald?' exclaimed Marlene.

'A couple of nizgals from Alf Jenkins,' said Donald.

'Whatever's a nizgal?' Marlene retreated hastily from the bag while Donald lifted out two pink and wriggling piglets.

'Maybe you'd call them runts,' he said. 'They're the tiny ones from the litter and won't thrive if they're left with the sow. We'll put them in the old sty and tiddle them along. I'll show you how to look after them.'

Marlene looked doubtfully at the little pigs, who were a miserable skinny little pair with their tails hanging straight.

'We'll soon have 'em going along nicely,' said Donald. 'I'll put 'em in the sty now with a nice warm bed of straw and I've got a cow coming this afternoon so we'll have plenty of milk for them, after you've skimmed it for butter.'

'Who said anything about me milking a cow?' asked Marlene in amazement. 'I've never had anything to do with one in my life!'

'You're never too old to learn,' said Donald, knowing full well that Marlene was still on shaky ground after the episode with the bathroom and intending to use his advantage to the full.

'If I am to milk the cow and feed the pigs, what happens to the money we make from milk and butter and the sale of the pig?' Marlene asked, getting to the heart of the matter at the outset.

'You'll have all the money from the cow, m'dear, and we'll share the pig money for you will feed them but I will do the cleaning out and help to supply the food. Tis only fair that way.'

'Tater's found this beautiful Guernsey cow going very cheaply as the owner doesn't want to be bothered milking it any more. 'Tis a lovely animal and he'll be bringing it along this afternoon. The milking pail and stool my dear old mother used to use are still hanging up there in the shed and I'll get them out for you and we'll have lovely fresh milk and farmhouse butter and enough left over to sell and to feed the pigs. 'Tis a very economical idea all round.'

'I might have guessed Tater had something to do with it,' Marlene muttered bitterly as she retreated to the kitchen, 'as if I haven't got enough to do already.'

Just before three o'clock Tater came ambling down the lane with the cow plodding meekly along beside him. It was an attractive golden and white colour with curly horns and a keenly intelligent eye. Tater tied the cow up in the barn ready for Marlene to milk it, and he hung around hopefully, full of good advice, but Marlene wasn't going to let him know how ignorant she was of cows and milking and waited until he had left before scouring out the milking pail and making her way to the barn. She fetched some hay and put it under the cow's nose and timidly approached the cow's side with her stool and pail, sitting down and stroking the cow softly. The cow responded by giving Marlene a stinging flick around the ear with its tail and looked around at her enquiringly.

Marlene pulled tentatively at the cow's teats squirting tiny amounts into the bucket. The cow waited until Marlene had settled down before she kicked the bucket over, and when Marlene had painstakingly managed to get a pint of milk in the bottom she picked up her hind leg and put her foot right in the pail. She then arched her back and a stream of yellow urine followed by a series of runny cowpats landed right by Marlene. A final flick of the tail around Marlene's head and the cow looked around enquiringly with an expression of bland innocence on her face.

It was the last straw for Marlene who had a miserable time putting up with Donald's jibes over the past few weeks. There was no way she was going to let a wretched cow get the better of her. She exploded with fury, and picking up the cow's hay and tossing it to one side Marlene tied the cow's tail to its back leg and finding a piece of rope she tied the cow's back legs together. She then left the cow standing there, trussed up like a chicken while she went back to the house to scald her pail again and make a cup of tea. When she returned she sluiced the manure away and glared angrily at the cow.

'Right.' She fumed. 'Now see if you can get your foot in the bucket again.'

She sat down and began to pull hard on the cow's teats, shouting at the cow each time it fidgeted and the cow responded by letting her milk flow and stood placidly until Marlene had finished. Little did either of them realise that it was the beginning of a lasting friendship between them that produced large quantities of rich milk which Marlene turned into golden farmhouse butter, much in demand at the market.

Donald was quietly surprised when he came home to find the cow grazing contentedly in the house paddock and Marlene in the house with a good pail full of milk. He knew perfectly well that the cow was only sold cheaply because it was known to be a mean and difficult beast to milk, and he had been anticipating quite a bit of trouble before Marlene would be able to milk it successfully.

'Well you had better show me what you want done with all this milk now I've got it,' said Marlene who suspected that Tater and Donald knew all about the cow's nasty habits. Donald hurried out to the shed to fetch the pans his mother had used for setting the cream and the old butter churn and brought them into the kitchen to scrub and scald. He poured off a large jug of milk for the house and set the pans on the stone slab in the pantry in the cool, pouring the milk into one.

'You leave that until the cream has risen and set and then you skims it off for butter and the pigs and chickens can have the skimmed milk. 'Tis good for scones and baking too,' he added. 'I'll show you how to make the butter when we've got enough cream to make a batch.'

He disappeared into the cupboard under the stairs and unearthed a pair of wooden butter pats and some moulds for shaping the butter and before many days were out Marlene had added milking and butter making to her daily chores and had learned how to feed the two flourishing little piglets who now carried their tails in tight little curls.

Chapter Twenty-Six
Sweet Revenge

Tater was bitterly disappointed to hear that the cow was behaving well. He had been hoping to expand his repertoire in the Red Lion to include a demonstration of Marlene milking the cow.

The knowledge that Tater persisted in his parody of her incident with the vicar irked Marlene and she spent a lot of time pondering how to get even with him while she worked at her chores around the house and garden. At last she hit on an idea that might work and cause him embarrassment in the pub, the very place where he was embarrassing her.

While she was working in the apple fields in the autumn Marlene had listened to the local women chatting and the talk had got around to an old fellow who had lived in the district all his life. He had worked as a casual labourer on the local farms, much in the way that Donald did, and in his spare time he was a fanatical gardener. He reckoned he could tell any seed by looking

152

at it or tasting it. When some of the land-girls working with him had put together a packet of mice muck and asked him to identify it, old Len had rubbed it in his work hardened hands and then put some in his mouth to chew. He spat it out saying, ''Tis mice muck, girls,' before taking a swig of his cider and finishing his crust of bread and corner of fat ham which he had brought for his mid-day meal.

Tater had recently taken to boasting that he could tell any seed by its appearance or taste and Marlene decided to play the same trick on him. She gathered up a good quantity of mice muck from the shelves in the potting shed, waited until Donald was out for the day and set it on the stove in an old lid to harden. She opened the door and windows to get rid of the smell and when it rattled like dried seed she let it cool before donning an old pair of gardening gloves and trimming the little pellets until they looked for all the world like little black seeds. She took a great deal of care to get it right. Once she was satisfied Marlene put the 'seeds' in an old envelope, rolled it up and put it by the clock on the mantelpiece until Sunday.

Donald like most of the men in the village went to the pub on a Sunday morning to have a pint and a chat and maybe a game of darts. He then came home to a good Sunday roast and put his feet up and snoozed in the afternoon. It was quite a regular thing and Tater would be in the pub for sure.

Marlene waited until Donald was just on his way out of the door then took the envelope down from the shelf.

'While you're in the pub, Donald, give these seeds to Tater and ask him to let me know what they are. I've been turning out the potting shed and I can't for the life of me work out what they are, and I don't want to waste time on them if they're not what we want, do I?'

Donald took the envelope and slipped in the breast pocket of his sports jacket alongside his darts. He looked neat and well cared for as he walked up the lane in his sports jacket with a new pair of corduroy trousers and Marlene's hand knitted jumper, a different man from the scruffy down at heel individual he had been before his marriage.

When Donald walked into the bar at the pub he found it packed as there was a darts match on between Millbrook and Rawton. He elbowed his way to the bar and ordered his usual half pint of bitter, greeting and nodding to people as he went and picking up his drink he made his way over to where Tater was involved in the darts match.

'How be ya.' He nodded to Tater and handed him Marlene's envelope. 'Marlene sent these,' he said. 'Reckons she can't work out what they are and wondered if you could tell her.'

Tater tipped some of the little black pellets in his hand and rubbed them thoughtfully. His eyesight was not as good as it once was and in the dim light of the bar he found it hard to see them properly. The men around him stopped talking and watched his as he tossed the seeds into his mouth and chewed them thoughtfully. Suddenly, he spat vigorously into the fire and took a deep swig of beer.

'What do you reckon they are then, Tater?' asked Ron Williams.

'Mice muck!' said Tater tersely and turned back to his game of darts, trying to ignore the wave of laughter around him.

'I reckon she had you that time, boy,' said Donald grinning. 'That'll teach you to make fun of her.'

Marlene had the dinner just ready as Donald came in through the kitchen door and the smell of roast lamb greeted him as he stepped in. Marlene could almost set the clock by him on a Sunday for he was a creature of habit and seldom came home earlier than one o'clock or later than ten minutes past.

'Many in the pub today, Donald?' she asked as she stirred the gravy.

'Ah, quite a few,' Donald replied, 'there was a darts match on with Rawton so there was quite a crowd.'

'Did you ask Tater about my seeds, then?' Marlene said casually, trying not to sound as if mattered at all.

'Ah.' Donald grinned again at the thought of Tater's disgusted face. 'He said it was mice muck, girl.'

'Did he now,' said Marlene, 'and how did he find that out?'

'He put some in his mouth and chewed it,' said Donald chuckling.

'Good!' said Marlene in a deeply satisfied voice. 'That's just what I was hoping he would do!'